KILLS MANY QUICKLY

THE RETURN OF TRAVIS WALKER - BOOK ONE

DAVE P. FISHER

1

Travis Walker stood at the window of the house's second floor, watching a crew pole a heavily laden flatboat against the current of the Missouri River. It was slow going, in the several minutes he had been standing there, they had made only a few yards of progress. He shifted his feet and could feel the softening of the floor under his boots, and wondered how long before the floor gave way.

The house had stood for the last twenty-four years, ever since William Clark built it as part of the fort meant for trade with the Osage Indians. Clark, and his partner, Merriwether Lewis, had led the Corp of Discovery into the new Louisiana Purchase. On the way they had decided this high ground overlooking the river would be a prime spot for a trading fort. Travis agreed, it was a prime spot.

It was still an operating fort in '22, when him and the boys had come west. That was the last year it had operated. In the ensuing ten years, it had badly deteriorated. The fort's palisade of logs was breaking down. The corner guard towers, one was down, the other leaning critically. The main house he occupied had been built soundly, with two stories, and a huge stone fireplace on each end wall. Still, even it was crumbling. The second-floor's balcony roof had succumbed to the ravages of rain and snow, and fallen in. The roof over the ground floor's porch was sagging, but he had propped up several feet of it over the entrance door.

He turned, and made his way down the creaking stairway, the wooden steps bowing under his two-hundred and twenty pounds. Coming to the ground floor, he thought to check his dry goods in the kitchen pantry. Shaking each cloth sack, he estimated he needed coffee, flour, and beans. He had the last haunch of a deer hanging in one of the deserted barracks. He needed to make a trip out to Columbia to buy more staples. He also needed to hunt, but the will to go out was not in him today.

The fire, fueled with oak and cottonwood, was glowing under the battered, blackened coffee pot. Wrapping a rag around the pot's handle, he poured the last of the thick coffee into his cup, and removed the pot from the fire. Walking across the room, he opened the door, ducked his head to exit the small doorway, and stepped out onto the porch.

He stood there looking over the dilapidated fort. His blue roan, the Nez Perce stud, he had traded for at the Pierre's Hole rendezvous in '29, grazed on the grass that had grown up over what was once only trampled dirt. Pierre's Hole, was the last rendezvous he and the boys, had attended, before he got the idea to go south. He shook the thought out of his head. He had spent too much time reliving, and regretting, that move. He finished the coffee, then went back inside.

He needed to do something with his life. It was two years ago that he crawled into this hole. To hide from the cruelty of the world, to avoid all people, and to leave the mountains to other men. How long would he keep this up? How long *could* he keep this up? One day, the house would fall down flatter than his spirit. It would die, but he wouldn't. Then, what?"

He picked up his rifle, powder horn, and possibles bag. He was going hunting. He had brooded long enough for one day. He left the house, and walked across the compound yard. Leaving the perimeter walls of the old fort, he crossed the trail. It was still used, but not to the extent it once was. It led to Santa Fe, in the Spanish lands. He had never been down there, and had no desire to do so. He moved on into the woods.

. . .

THE FLICKERING FLAME of a single candle, stuck in a metal holder, cast a dancing glow on the walls of the room. The fire, licking up around slabs of oak, cast another glow that melded with the candle's light. A turkey hung on the spit over the flames. He had not found a deer today, but the turkey that wandered out in front of him would do. Travis sat in a chair, staring into the fire, just as he done for the past six-hundred nights. Images, branded deeply in his mind paraded before him. He wanted to banish them, drive them away forever, but in so doing he would drive away their faces as well.

Taking hold of the turkey's leg, he cut half of the bird off. He bounced the hot meat from one hand to the other, until it was cool enough to eat. He bit off a chunk. Sitting there alone, in the silence of his wounded heart, he ate. Not because he was hungry, but because he had to eat. In his memories, he could hear the laughter of the trappers gathered around a fire. Yarns, were spun, few of which were true, but they were fun. He finished eating the bird, then went to the bed, and rolled into his blankets to spend another night filled with dreams, and nightmares.

ON OCCASION, men bound for the mountains, or a wagon traveling to some point on the Santa Fe Trail would stop to look at the old fort. Outside of the compound, the grass was rich, making good graze for the horses and mules while the people took a rest. Some spent the night on the outside. Those that sought to camp inside the compound, grazing their stock on the grass, that belonged to his roan, were quickly sent back out. No one argued with the big man. It was easier to simply move to the outside.

Men heading for the mountains heard about the trapper who had taken up residence in old Fort Osage. Some had known him before, knew his story, and left him to his own company. There was nothing of interest in the old fort that would cause any of them to intrude on Travis Walker's solitary life.

Travis walked out of the house and looked around. The sun was indicating mid-afternoon. He heard horses and arguing men approaching from the trail. He hoped they would simply ride on by, he would run them off if they didn't. The idea that travelers had to come into the old compound in the first place was irritating. Some wanted to stay in the shelter of the abandoned barrack rooms. They could stay outside, the last thing he wanted was people around who he had to keep an eye on to be sure they didn't steal anything of his.

The arguing, sound of shifting tack, and a good many horse hooves striking the ground drew closer. It was a large party, and their arguing did not bode well for them being friendly. He went back into the house, took up his rifle, and watched through the glassless window frame.

Ten men rode into the compound. He grumbled a

curse; he didn't need a party of antagonistic troublemakers camping in his front yard. They were directing their wrath toward a man on a bay horse, who seemed to be injured as he slumped in the saddle.

The group began to dismount. That was it! Travis stormed out of the house, rifle in hand, a Bowie knife on his belt. "Don't bother gettin' down!" he shouted across the yard. "You ain't stayin' here."

The men looked at him, "We'll stay where we please," one of the men called back.

"Take your quarrelin' pack of dogs out of here – now!"

A man with a full red beard, and long matching hair, stepped toward him, "You won't be tellin' us nothin'," he said in a Scottish brough. "If you don't like us stayin' here, we'll just kill yuh, and take it."

"You will, will you!" Travis took a big step closer to red beard.

Red beard backed up a step. "You can't take all of us."

"Think not, huh? Stick around and find out."

One of the men who was off his horse moved at him, "I'll find out right now," he growled.

As the man closed in, Travis snapped the rifle up, striking the man hard across the side of the head with the heavy barrel. The blow stopped the charge. With one hand on the barrel, one on the stock, Travis slammed the rifle across the man's nose, smashing it in a spray of blood. He screamed and fell to his knees, hands clasped over his face as the blood oozed between his fingers.

Travis looked the group over, "Who's next?"

Another man pulled a six-inch knife, "I'll cut you to ribbons."

Holding the rifle in his left hand, Travis pulled the Bowie with a twelve-inch blade. "Come on."

The man's knife looked tiny compared to the Bowie. He stopped and stared at the big knife.

"Come on," Travis taunted. "Cut me to ribbons."

The men stood still, looking at him as if weighing the odds of rushing him.

"You're a pack of gutless, bully coyotes," Travis said. "Get out."

At that moment a man, dressed in buckskins, rode into the compound. "What are you doin'?" he shouted at them. "I said, keep goin'. We don't have time to dally around."

Travis' eyes narrowed at the buckskin clad man; he was a mountain man. It had been a few years, but he knew him. "Luther Monk!" he called out.

Monk had not paid attention to the man confronting the gang, but his attention locked on him now. His eyes widened with recognition, and fear.

"Not a bit surprised you're leadin' this pack of coyotes. You've got ten seconds to get out of here, before I blow you off that horse."

"Now, take it easy Walker, you got me all wrong." Monk pleaded.

"I got you just right, and now, it's seven seconds. Keep runnin' your mouth."

"I'm just guidin' them into the mountains, that's all."

"Sure, to murder and steal. Four seconds."

Monk began to show panic, he knew Travis Walker would shoot him, he had done it before. "Get on your horses," he snapped at the men.

Red beard turned to look at him, "Why?"

"Don't argue, just do it," Monk cried out.

"He can't take all of us," red beard argued.

"Yes, he can!" Monk snapped. "He's done it with more. Get on your horse, or I'm leaving you right here." Monk reined his horse around, and kicked him into a run out of the compound.

Two men helped the one with the smashed nose up on his horse. His face and hands were covered in blood. Red beard looked at him, then turned to sneer at Travis," We'll be seeing you again."

"That would be a real bad idea," Travis said. "Your time is up – get out." He cocked back the hammer on the Hawken and leveled it at red beard."

The men quickly mounted. "You can keep this one," red beard said as he pushed the wounded man off his horse. The man hit the ground hard, letting out a cry of pain. They rode out after Monk.

Travis looked down at the man on the ground. His horse walking further into the compound. "What's your problem?" he said to the man.

"I've been shot," he whispered between gasps.

"I'm sure it wasn't by accident. Coyotes like you get shot for a reason. You can crawl into one of those barracks, and die."

The man stared at Travis, "Aren't you going to help me?"

Travis held a cold look on him, "Don't see any reason why I should. You run with a pack of coyotes; you can expect to get shot like one." He turned and walked back to the house.

Stopping at the porch he saw the man crawl into one of the barracks. He looked past him to the opening where gates had once stood. "Luther Monk," he said aloud. "I wonder what he's up to? With that pack of coyotes, it can't be anything good."

2

In St. Charles, the fur house of Martin Ouimette was a two-story brick, situated on Main Street, overlooking the Missouri River. The Ouimette Fur Company traded mainly with independent trappers. The headquarters of the Rocky Mountain Fur Company, located twenty-five miles downstream in St. Louis, did a bigger business due to their excursions into the Rocky Mountains, still the Ouimette Fur Company enjoyed a good profit.

The independent, or free trappers, as they called themselves, to hold them apart from the company owned trappers, preferred to trade with Ouimette because he was once a free trapper himself. Martin Ouimette was Metis, from the Lake Winnipeg, Red River country of Canada. The French trusted him, because he was one of them. The Indians, who came downriver to sell their pelts, trusted him because he was half Indian. Unlike many fur buyers, he was honest in his dealings, and that drove business to him.

The stories brought back by the men returning from the Rocky Mountains regarding the ruthless tactics of the big fur companies, were not complimentary. The owners of the big companies were often under-handed in destroying their competitors in order to take the biggest share of the beaver trade. The accounts did not encourage the trappers who worked to the north, to trade with their fur houses in St. Louis. By that concern, Martin Ouimette profited.

TWO FRENCH TRAPPERS, Remi and Paul Marier, stood in the lower level of the Ouimette Fur House; they were watching Martin sort through their collection of furs. He spread the dried pelts across two large tables, sorting them into piles. Beaver, otter, muskrat, mink, and fox lay before his expert. appraising eye.

"These are fine pelts, my friends," Martin said. "Where are you from?"

"Lake Michigan country," Remi replied. "We were born and raised near Durham, in the Newcastle District of Canada; we know everyone there. Our family is a big one around there, all in the fur trade, however, Paul, and I, grew tired of being forced to sell our furs to Hudson Bay for a portion of what they were worth. We moved down to the

American side, and trapped the streams flowing into the big lake for a few years. There, we sold our pelts in Saginaw, for a much better price than Hudson Bay."

"You are a long way from Saginaw, now," Martin remarked.

"We are working our way west," Remi said. "These pelts came from the streams along the Illinois River."

Martin nodded, "That is closer to here. How far west are you going?"

"To the Rocky Mountains," Paul answered. "We have heard that there is a wealth of furs there, and beaver number like geese. We could do well."

"The beaver will not last forever," Martin said. "Hundreds of trappers have gone into that country over the past several years, ever since Ashley lead his brigade of trappers in eighteen-twenty-four." He grinned, "You had better hurry while there are still beaver left."

"Have you been to the Rocky Mountains?" Paul asked.

Martin shook his head, "It has not interested me."

"You are a trapper, no?"

"I was. I am a businessman, now. My wilderness days are behind me."

"It would seem to me, a trapper would be excited about the Rocky Mountains," Paul persisted.

"Not, this one," Martin remarked.

"You are Metis, I understand," Remi broke in to stop his brother from badgering Martin.

"That is right. My mother is Cree."

"Did you come from the Lake Winnipeg country?"

"Yes, on the Red River. I brought my wife and child down from there. I trapped my way down the Red River, then the St. Peters River, then down the Mississippi River, to St. Louis. It took three years; my second daughter was born on the way. I started this company in eighteen-eighteen."

"The thought of venturing into the Rocky Mountains, has truly never interested you?" Paul broke in.

"I would not leave my family, and business, for a venture. Besides, if I did, who would free trappers, as yourselves, sell their furs to? Most are not interested in selling to the fur houses in St. Louis, run by businessmen from the East."

"Paul!" Remi snapped, "Stop annoying Monsieur Ouimette! He has already told you that he has no interest in going to the Rocky Mountains. That is enough, now!"

Martin smiled, "He is young, and excited. Every young man thinks that all must be excited for the same things he is."

"Still, I offer my apologies for my young brother," Remi said.

Martin waved his hand, "It is fine. I have a price for your pelts."

The brothers nodded their agreement. "It is a fair price," Remi said.

Martin left the room, going into his office. He returned with the money and counted it out for them.

Remi picked it up, "Thank you, Monsieur Ouimette."

"Good luck in the Rocky Mountains," Martin said. "You can sell your furs at a rendezvous, or bring them back to me for a better price."

"We will see," Remi replied with a smile. "Before we leave, I want to pass on some information. Do you know Portage de Sioux, on the Mississippi River?"

Martin nodded, "Yes, I often go there to buy pelts."

"There was a robbery in Portage de Sioux, a few days ago," Remi went on. "A fur trader was murdered, and his furs stolen. It is the talk in every camp and tavern. It is said to be a gang of river pirates murdering and robbing all the way down the river. Some men have seen them and say there are eight or ten in the gang.

Paul broke in, "We heard a Courier from Lake Winnipeg, telling the crowd in a tavern, that this gang is from the Red River area, they are thugs for Hudson Bay. They were involved in destroying Fort Gibraltar, and attacking the Northwest Company men. He was also telling an account of the Hudson Bay Governor attacking a party of Metis, who were working for the Northwest Company. They were carrying pemmican to Fort William. They fired on the Metis, but the Metis killed several, and won the battle. The story was very interesting. Do you know of this situation, since you are Metis, and came from there? Is it true?"

Martin stiffened a bit, then replied, "Yes, I have heard of it. I have no reason to doubt the Courier's story." He looked back at Remi, "Who was the murdered fur merchant?"

"An Englishman, named Brian Harper."

"I know him. We were not friends, but mutual acquaintances in the business. We met a few times at the fur auctions. It is a great tragedy; he had a wife and children. Are the authorities looking for them?"

Remi shrugged, "I suppose, but how do you find men who do not want to be found?"

"There is only so much the sheriff can do," Martin agreed.

"Such men do not care who they kill," Remi said. "This gang robs and murders, but they know fur buyers carry a good deal of money, as well as the furs. I am telling you, because you are a fur merchant, and you travel. You must be careful."

Martin frowned as he considered the warning. "Yes, I will be careful."

Remi and Paul left the room. Martin held the frown as he considered what Remi had told him. A gang of reprobate thieves and murderers, who once worked for Hudson Bay. He might recognize these men if he saw them, but even if he did not, he knew the kind of men they were. There had been no reason for Governor Semple's thugs to open fire on the North-west Company's men. The thugs had cheered when they opened fire on the Metis, however, they did not cheer long.

He shook the thought from his head, he had work to do. Worrying about these cutthroats would not get him ready for the auction in two days. There were hundreds of pelts to grade and organize. He was going to realize a good profit as the European markets were still demanding fur.

The afternoon passed quickly as he prepared the pelts. No trappers came in to disrupt his work. He was examining a prime red fox pelt when the door opened. He looked up to see his wife, Odette, coming in with their two daughters. They were dressed to be out in the city.

Martin smiled at them, "Where are you going?"

"We are returning," Odette said with a light laugh. "We went out the back stairway. You were buying furs from those two men, and we did not want to disturb you."

Martin looked them over, and the packages they carried. "Yes, I see the packages now, my mind was occupied adding numbers." He grinned, "Did you spend all my money?"

"Only most of it," Odette replied with a smile.

Martin let out a theatrical moan, "I will have to make sure the pelts sell well, or I cannot afford to keep you."

Odette feigned shock, "You would cast me away so easily?"

Martin looked at his sixteen-year-old daughter, Sharice,

"Maybe, just this one. As she gets older, she will cost me more."

"Papa!" Sharice exclaimed, with a laugh. "I thought you loved me!"

"I do love you, dear one. I will apprentice you to a tailor, a kindly gesture on my part."

"That is a kindly gesture, father?"

"Yes," Martin replied as if surprised by her question. "I could apprentice you to a washerwoman."

Sharice gave him a sly grin, "If I brought you a sugar bun from the baker, would you let me stay?"

"Oh, absolutely."

Sharice removed a sugar bun, wrapped in brown paper, from her basket, and handed it to him. "I love you."

Martin gave her a hug, "Thank you."

"How about me, papa?" Thirteen-year-old Yvonne asked.

Martin gave her a comical, but serious look, "Did you spend my money?"

"No, papa, I did not spend any money."

"Oh, that is good, you can stay."

Yvonne giggled, "Mama spent your money for me."

"Oh, she did, did she," Martin said while trying not to laugh. "Your mother and I will have to have a talk."

The girls laughed, "Love you," they shouted together, as they ran up the stairs leading to their home on the second floor.'

Martin watched them, as he held the sugar bun. He looked at Odette, "What did *you* bring me from the city?"

"Just this." She kissed him. "Dinner will be at five." She followed the girls up the stairs.

"Okay, you can stay, too," he called after her.

Odette turned and gave him a curtsey, "Thank you, me lord." She laughed and continued up the stairs.

Martin laughed, as he went back to figuring the value of the pelts.

THE FOLLOWING MORNING, the pelts for the auction were stored in the rear of the building. Room up front was available for any new pelts that came in before the auction. He was sweeping the floor when two men opened the door and walked in. Martin stopped, and studied the two. One man had his arms wrapped around a bundle of beaver pelts; the other had a variety of other pelts pressed against his chest. Their faces were barely visible above the furs.

"Are you Mr. Ouimette?" the man with the beaver pelts asked.

"I am," Martin answered. He leaned the broom against the wall, and walked to the grading counter.

"We have furs to sell, and we understand you're the best man to sell them to."

"Yes, I am always interested in pelts. Lay them on the table here."

The men dropped the bundles on the table, giving Martin the first opportunity to see their faces and clothes. They were dressed like Englishmen, not trappers. One was brown-haired and had the look of a Frenchman. The man who had spoken, held his attention, though he tried not to show it, but something stirred in his stomach. The man bore a full, bright red beard, and long, greasy hair of the same color. He was familiar, as if he had seen him before, but he couldn't place where that might have been.

Many of the trappers who came in were equally dirty, and unkempt. It was not unnatural, or surprising, that these men were in such a state. Some of the best trappers could not be distinguished from the furs in their arms. Still, there was something unsettling about this pair, as their attention roved over the room, rather than on the pelts in front of them.

He began to sort through the pelts. As he always did, he separated them by species. What his expert eye detected, was the way each pelt had been skinned, fleshed, and dried. Every trapper had his own fashion in preparing pelts, and it was their hand that clearly handled each pelt in their possession. Some were handled poorly, too much fat left on that burned the hair, and rendered the pelt of low value. Others, had been prepared at the hand of an artist. These pelts, had been handled by several different men, not just the two men who had them.

In an effort to learn something of the men, he said, "These are nicely handled."

The red beard man smiled, "Thank you, we pride ourselves in our work."

Martin detected the accent of a Scotsman.

"Yes, I can see that. Where have you been trapping?"

"All over," the man replied.

Martin knew that some men had no problem talking about what streams they had trapped on. Other men, were secretive about it, not wishing to divulged the place in fear others would take their traplines over. He didn't press the man further.

While he graded the pelts he wondered if these men were the murderers and fur thieves. How else would they end up with such a variety of handling styles. The other thing that struck him was, if these were the men who robbed Brian Harper, there would be far more pelts than these few here. Who bought the rest of the pelts? As if making idle chatter, he asked, "Did you trap them all yourself, or buy some from the Indians?"

Red beard narrowed his eyes at him, "Why do you ask?"

Martin shrugged, "It is more profitable to buy some from the Indians, and trap some. You can end up with more money if you do. Many trappers do."

The men gave a quick glance to each other, "We did buy some from the Indians, and a few from other trappers who didn't want to come into the city."

Perhaps, these men were trappers who bought some of the pelts after all. Besides, the gang was supposed to consist of eight or ten men. As he calculated the value, Odette came down the stairs. "Oh," she said, "I did not know you were transacting business. I will talk to you later." She turned and went back up the stairs. The eyes of the two men followed her.

Their attention quickly turned back to Martin as he quoted a price.

"We'll take it," red beard replied.

Martin walked back into his office. Taking the money from the strongbox, he returned to where the men stood. He saw them looking up the stairway, but they looked back at him as he approached. He counted the money out on the table.

Taking it up, red beard smiled at Martin, "Thank you, Mr. Ouimette, it was a pleasure doin' business with an honest man." They turned and walked out the door.

Martin waited until they closed the door, then hurried to it. Cracking it open he could see the two men walking down the street. No other men joined them. Maybe he was just imaging things because the gang was prominent on his mind. Still, there was something about them that disturbed him.

The Scot preyed on his memory; he had seen him before. The Courier in the tavern said they had been with the Hudson Bay thugs who destroyed the Northwest

Company fort at Red River. It was possible red beard was part of the Red River Colony. It was a load of Scotsmen, sent by the Earl of Selkirk to squat on the Indian and Metis lands of the Red and Assiniboine Rivers. That had caused a great conflict. There were free Scots in charge of those indentured, and some were employed by Hudson Bay. They all represented the Earl's interests, and often pitted themselves against the Metis. Could this man have been one of the thugs, or did he simply remind him of those days? He closed the door, yet the uneasy feeling remained.

3

The morning came in with a drizzling rain. Martin stood in the front room of the second floor where they lived. It was not a large building, however, there were several rooms for the family to live comfortably. He was staring out the window, to the river. He had worked hard since settling in St. Charles to give his family a good life.

The fur business was lucrative, but how long would it last? To the Indian, fur was clothing, and trade goods. To the trapper, it was supplies to keep them in the mountains, and the money. To the wealthy in Europe and eastern America, it was fashion. Fashion dictated the value of fur. Fashion was fickle, it had a bad habit of changing the moment a new thing came along. What would he do once the fur fashion ended? It was something to expect, as nothing lasted forever. He would have to find some other commodity to deal in.

Through the rain spattered window he watched two flatboats being poled up the river. Laden with boxes and crates stacked high, and wide, he knew they were trade goods for the Rocky Mountains. Every spring, the boats were laboriously poled up the powerful Missouri River. It was a slow process fighting against the current, yet they persisted in making the trek. Wealth, or bankruptcy, waiting in the far-off mountains. The company who got to the trapper rendezvous first would profit, the slow would lose, thus the stories of companies doing whatever was needed to be the first.

He had spent many years trapping and hunting the woods and streams of the north country. He had to admit, there were days when he missed the life. He was a good trapper, and he loved the woods. Watching the flatboats was like seeing the geese winging through the sky, there was an itch to follow them.

He pushed the thoughts away by telling himself, he had no desire for the Rocky Mountains. He was tired of the cold, and there was more money to be made buying the pelts, then catching them. Those were merely justifications to settle the argument in his mind, and he knew it. The real reason he left the woods and traplines was for Odette, and his daughters, they kept him in St. Charles, by choice, not force. Odette had spent years living out of trapper camps, without a complaint. Now, she had earned an easier life.

The thought of them brought back the previous day, and the two men. The dirty, red bearded one still stuck in his mind. He had seen how they looked at the stairs after Odette had ascended them. They weren't studying the architecture; they were looking after her. It was not unusual for a man to let his eyes linger for a moment on a beautiful woman. Odette was typical of the French women, dark-brown hair, brown eyes, and comely face. A man's attention may linger a moment on her, but to stare after she was gone, was inappropriate.

He could have challenged the men for looking after her, but they could have easily argued that they were not. Had they said anything about her, then he had grounds to challenge them, but to look? They could say they were looking at something else. There was a time when he was quick to fight, yet he was also one to never falsely accuse a man of wrongdoing. To accuse required proof, or a fight, or duel, was in order by the accused.

Odette suddenly appeared beside him. She looked out the window to see the flatboats on the river. "Do you miss it?" she asked.

Martin turned his head to look at her, "Miss, what?"

Odette looked into his eyes, "I know you too well, my love. I see the trails and waterways in your eyes. There is a longing in you to be back out on them."

Martin shook his head, "No, I am content here. Besides, you have earned this good life. The many years you slept on the cold, frozen ground, following me in pursuit of fur. Cooking over an open fire. Days when there was only beaver meat, or deer, to eat because the staples had run out, and we were far from a post to buy more. I have had my years doing what I wanted, now you will have your years of an easy life. A warm bed, warm house, no shortage of food."

She took his hand in hers, "I would do it again, for the love I have for you."

Martin held her eyes, "I know you would, that is why I would never ask it of you."

"I know." She looked out the window to the river, "Many times, I think back on our early years on the Red River. Living with the Metis, and the Cree, Nakoda, and Ojibwe. The cabin we had, and the birth of Sharice. Those were happy days for me. That was before the trouble."

Martin's face darkened, "Yes, the Earl of Selkirk, and his Red River colony. Macdonell's, Pemmican Proclamation. The day I went with Cuthbert Grant, and the others, to run the blockade to deliver pemmican to our friends. That ended our home on the Red River, and set us adrift."

"We have had a good home here for ten years, and a successful business. You have done wonderfully for us. Let the past, be in the past."

"Yes," Martin agreed. Yet, he knew the past, especially

one with a violent story, had a way of coming back when least expected. Was the red bearded Scotsman part of that? What made him different from the many other trappers who came into the fur house, that he would so control his thoughts?

Sharice and Yvonne came into the room, "We are ready for school," Sharice announced.

Odette looked at them, "It is raining, put on your coats, or you will catch your death."

Odette usually walked the girls to school. He had not told his family about the gang of cutthroats on the loose, but until they were apprehended, he would walk them to school. "I will walk with you today, girls," Martin said.

"I can walk with them," Odette said. "I am not a sugar plum to melt in the rain."

"Oh, I just feel like a walk in the rain this morning," Martin replied.

"As you wish," Odette said. "I do not mind staying in a nice, warm house."

Martin smiled, "Get your coats on, girls."

The girls ran for their coats. Martin walked down the stairs to the fur house. A minute later he came back up with his coat on.

Odette studied the disturbed look on his face, then saw one of his coats hanging on a peg by the back door. Why had he gone downstairs for one, when a coat was right here? She walked up to him, and pulled back his unbuttoned coat, tucked into his belt was a pistol. The weight of the pocket said he had a powder and ball pouch in it.

He silently met her questioning eyes. She glanced around to see if the girls were close, then asked, "What is it? What is it you fear about us going out?"

Martin did not reply.

"I see you are troubled. When you return, you will tell me what it is. I cannot be prepared, if I do not know what it is."

Martin nodded, "I will tell you."

The girls returned wearing their coats. Martin quickly buttoned his coat to hide the pistol. They all walked down the stairs, and out to the street.

Odette watched them until they were out of sight. It took a lot to trouble Martin, he was a man of courage, and always sure of himself, but protective of her and the girls. If he was disturbed, it had to involve them.

Odette was sitting at the table when Martin came back up the interior stairs from the fur house. He carried a different, but duplicate pistol, and pouch, in his hands. He placed them on the table. "Do you remember how to use this?" he asked.

Odette nodded, "Yes."

"This one is loaded already, but tell me how it works."

"Pull back the hammer until it locks. Put a cap on the nipple. Pull the trigger. Blow down the barrel to remove any embers. Pour a measure of powder in, then a patch and ball. Ram it down with the ramrod. Hammer back, cap on, fire. Now, tell me what is going on?"

Martin sat down. "There is a roving gang of cutthroats in the area. Reports have it there are eight to ten of them. They murdered a fur merchant, and stole his furs, in Portage de Sioux the other day. They are reported to have been murdering and robbing their way down the Mississippi."

"I understand that they could target you, with your furs, and going armed is wise, but why are you so worried about the girls and I?"

"Yesterday, you came down the stairs, and saw me buying pelts from two men. You then went back upstairs. Did you notice anything about the two men?"

"No, except they were very dirty."

"One had red hair and beard?"

Odette furrowed her brow to recall, then nodded, "Yes, it seemed so. What about him?"

"He was a Scot, and there was something familiar about him, but I could not put my finger on it."

"You met him before, perhaps?"

"I had a feeling, he was part of that Red River colony, and one of the thugs who worked for Hudson Bay, maybe one of those who attacked our group. I may be completely wrong, but I have the feeling the two of them are members of that gang. They showed a good deal of interest in the furs stacked for the auction, and ..."

Odette gave him a worried look, "And? Yes?"

"They showed interest in you, after you had gone up the stairs."

"Are you sure? They were not simply looking?"

"That is the problem, I am not sure, but all of my instincts tell me to be cautious. There is something about them. I will be all day, and late, tomorrow at the auction. I want you to put the girls in their room early, and be ready with the pistol. Should they come in, shoot them."

Odette shifted uncomfortably in her chair. "For, the girls' sake, I hope you are wrong, but I know, we must always be prepared. I will keep the pistol close, but I do not want to scare the girls."

"I understand. I will get home as soon as I can finish my business."

IN THE MORNING, Martin loaded the pelts in his wagon. It was a full load; he had done well with the free trappers. He said good bye to Odette and the girls, and left with a sense of dread. He did not want to make this trip, yet he had to sell at the spring auction if he expected to recoup his expenses. Should he wait until the fall auction, he would be competing against the big companies bringing thousands of pelts in from the Rocky Mountains. The bids would be much lower, due to the glut of fur to be purchased, and it would near ruin him.

It took him five hours to reach the St. Louis auction house. He met several of his friends and business acquaintance, who were there to either sell, or bid. These meetings, in the past, had been filled with good camaraderie, and rekindling of friendships. Today, he felt no joy, only apprehension.

His friend, Prisque Tremblay, a French trapper, turned fur buyer, met him at his wagon. They shook hands. "It has been a month since I last saw you," Prisque said, "How is Odette, and your lovely daughters?"

"They are well. Odette wanted me to make sure you came to visit. It has been too long since you ate at our table."

"I will be sure and make the trip." He lifted the tarp over Martin's furs, and looked over the hundreds of pelts. He let out a low whistle, "You have done well, Martin."

"It has been a good season for me," Martin replied. He looked at the furs, and wondered about red beard. Whose pelts were those he sold to him? Brian Harper's?"

Prisque studied his friend's concerned expression, "Martin, you look troubled?"

Martin frowned, "I am. Have you heard about the gang of robbers and cutthroats? They killed Brian Harper in Portage de Sioux."

"Yes. They have been the subject of a good deal of talk in my area. What about them?"

"I am worried about leaving my family alone with that gang of murderers on the loose."

"They prey on fur merchants. We have to be careful, but why would they bother your family?"

Martin let out a shaky sigh, "Two men, with the look of scoundrels about them, sold pelts to me a few days back. One was a man with red beard and long red hair, he spoke with a Scot accent. I am certain I have seen him before, and that thought has haunted me, because the memory was not a good one. They also saw Odette."

Prisque furrowed his brow, "I have heard the leader was a red-haired Scot."

Martin's face suddenly filled with fear. "I must get home, but my pelts, I must sell them."

"You must go, right now!" Prisque exclaimed. "I will take care of your pelts, and make sure you get the best price. Go. Go – now! Take one of your horses, you will travel faster."

"Thank you, Prisque. You are a true friend."

"I will bring your money in the morning, and pray that all will be safe at your house tonight."

Martin quickly unharnessed one of the pair of black horses. In the wagon, he always carried a bridle in the event he had to ride. The horses were a breed known as the Canadian Horse, strong for pulling a wagon, yet excellent as a riding horse. He quickly bridled the horse, and swung onto its back. He was an expert rider, either bareback, or with a saddle. Kicking the horse, he put him into a gallop back toward St. Charles.

The horse had speed and endurance, as Martin was only five feet-seven inches tall, he was not heavy for the big horse. The Canada Horse held to a gallop, or canter, for two miles, then Martin brought him down to a walk, to keep him from exhaustion. Once the horse had caught his breath, he put him into a gallop again. Three hours from St. Louis, he rode down Main Street.

Riding to the stable behind the house, he turned the horse into the stall. He would tend to him briefly, but first he had to see his family. He ran up the rear steps, taking them two at a time. Reaching the door, he turned the handle, finding it locked. It was supposed to be locked, which gave him a sense that all was well.

He wrapped his knuckles on the door. Waiting for several seconds, he heard Odette call out, "Who is there?"

"It is I, Martin."

Odette opened the door. Her expression showed surprise at seeing him. "I did not expect to see you until late tonight."

Martin walked in. He looked at Odette, who held the pistol in her hand. The girls were sitting at the table looking at him. Their faces showing concern.

"Prisque is taking care of my pelts. I had to come home."

Odette furrowed her brow, "You have learned something about these men, yes?"

"Yes." He glanced at the girls.

"I chose to tell them everything," Odette said. "I wanted them to be aware."

Martin nodded, "It is better that they know. Prisque told me, he heard that the red beard man who was here, is the leader of the cutthroat gang. If he is from the Hudson Bay crowd, that is why I know him. He must have been with the Red River colony, and one of Hudson Bay's thugs. I must have seen him, and it stuck in my mind."

"Do you think they will come back here?" Odette asked.

"I do not know, but he might remember me. I was there at the battle. I shot two of their men. They might have come for me."

"The Hudson Bay men attacked the Metis," Odette said. "You were defending yourselves."

"That does not matter to outlaws and scoundrels. They only see things, as they want to see them, through their evil eyes."

"I am glad you came home then," Odette said. "I feel safer with you here."

"Keep your pistol ready. We will watch for them. If they have targeted us, they know I went to St. Louis; they will think you are alone."

"I will make supper," Odette said. She walked into the kitchen.

"Father," Sharice said, looking up from her book."

Martin looked at her, "Yes?"

"Will those bad men hurt us?"

"I will not let them, dear one. I will kill them all if they come here."

Sharice gave him a smile, yet her eyes showed her fear, "I am happy you are home with us." She went back to reading.

Supper was eaten with little talk, as Martin kept his hearing strained for any unusual noises outside. Darkness fell, the girls were sent off to bed. Martin kept a single whale oil lamp lit on the table where he sat. The pistol lay on the table inches from his hand. He had put on his sheathed knife. In his time, he had been in fights, where the knife was the weapon. He knew how to wield it with lethal force.

Odette sat opposite from him, sewing on Yvonne's dress by the lamp light. She frequently glanced up at Martin to see his countenance focused on the unseen. She did not disturb him. She understood the importance of silence when enemies were about.

The clock on the fireplace mantle chimed nine o'clock. Martin cast a glance at it. Maybe, he had over-reacted in regards to the threat, however, had he stayed until the end of the auction, he would still be on his way back from St. Louis. He reminded himself that thinking the danger had passed, or it had been over emphasized, was the best way to be caught with your guard down.

The clock chimed ten. Odette stood up, "I am going to bed. Are you?"

"No. I intend to be on guard all night. If they are coming, this will be the night."

Odette kissed him, lightly, "I love you." She left the pistol on the table.

"I love you, too." He indicated the pistol, "Take it with you. If they get past me, you can still defend yourself."

She picked up the pistol, and walked into the bedroom.

Martin sat, tense, and waiting. His ears trained on every sound.

Another hour passed, he began to drift off to sleep, but caught himself. He stood, and walk around the room. He was standing when the sound of scuffing came from the rear stairs. He directed his attention to the sound. It came again. No other sounds, just the scuffing. Someone was climbing the stairs.

He felt he should warn Odette, and have her go in with the girls, but he didn't dare leave the doorway. The scuffing stopped, then came the turning of the door handle. Cocking the pistol, he held it in his right hand, the knife in his left.

With an abrupt crash, the door was smashed open, the metal parts flying across the room. The first man in was black-haired, behind him were others. Leveling the pistol, he shot the man in the chest. He fell back against the others, who shoved the dead man back through the doorway, and came at Martin in a rush. Dropping the empty pistol, he swung the knife, cutting into the first man, slicing back and forth across his arms.

There were more men than he had expected. They overwhelmed him, and beat him to the floor. The crush on him made it impossible to use the knife, or throw a punch. He jabbed as best he could into the mass of men who buried him in kicks and punches. He felt himself blacking out, but fought against it. He had to fight on. He had to stop them. The last sound he heard was the explosion of Odette's pistol.

4

Martin opened his eyes. Rain was falling in his face, and the sound of shouting men was all around him. Where was he? His head throbbed, and his chest ached, but his senses were coming back to him. His nostrils were filled with the smell of smoke. Something was burning. What was it?

He turned his head to see flames coming from a building. A line of men was on a stairway passing buckets of water up it. The water was being thrown into the building, then the buckets dropped down from the landing. Men were calling out instructions. With a burst of realization, he understood it was his house that was on fire.

He forced himself to sit up. He gaped in horror at the scene. Fire leapt from the upper floor windows, as the men fought the fire with buckets of water. He attempted to stand, but fell back down, his head spinning dizzily.

A man shouted, "Look it there, he's alive!"

Two men rushed up to him. One was Sheriff Mills' deputy, carrying a lantern. "We thought you were dead," he said to Martin. "We will get you to the hospital."

"No," Martin shouted. His voice sounded like it belonged to someone else. My wife, my babies, are in there. I must get them out."

The man looked at the deputy. "We got them out," the deputy said.

"Are they well? Are they injured?" Martin cried out. "Where are they?"

"We can talk about it after you are treated by a doctor," the deputy replied.

"No!" Martin shouted. "Tell me, now!" Tell Me!"

Sheriff Henry Mills knelt down beside Martin. "Mr. Ouimette," he paused, wiping his hand across his face.

Martin stared into his face, "Tell me."

Mills let out a shaky breath, "They are dead."

Shock filled Martin's face, "What? What?"

"They are dead, Mr. Ouimette. I am so very sorry. So sorry."

Martin began to wail in grief. "My babies," he cried out. "My Odette!" He screamed in agony, collapsed back on the ground, and wept. "I was not able to stop them. I tried. I tried."

Mills looked at his deputy, then back to Martin, "Tried to stop who, Mr. Ouimette?"

"The gang. The red beard man. There were too many."

Mills frowned, "You were attacked?"

"Yes," Martin wailed. "There were too many. I shot one, but there were too many."

Mills stared at Martin, "He has passed out." He shouted at one of the men, "Get an ambulance over here, immediately."

"We found a dead man, a street over," the deputy said to the sheriff. "He was shot. Could he be the one Martin shot?"

Mills gestured for the deputy to move away from Martin with him. "The bodies of the woman and children were burned, but not so badly. I want to look at them."

They walked to where the three bodies lay under blankets. He uncovered the woman. "Hold the lantern close to her." He looked at the charred body. "She has no clothes on. Her body is not so burned that her clothes would have burned off. He took a closer look at the body, then focused on the neck and head. "Lantern, closer!"

The deputy lowered the lantern.

Mills fingered her throat. "Her throat has been cut. A very thin line is there, see it?"

The deputy looked closer, "Yes, I see it. The blood would have flowed out, and burned away."

"The woman was molested, and then murdered," Mills said. "My, God!"

The deputy then uncovered the bodies of the children. Mills looked at them. Both girls were unclothed, and their throats cut. "My, God!" Mills cried out. "What manner of monsters were they?"

"Might have been that gang from up north," the deputy said. "They have been seen in these parts. It would fit what Martin said about there being too many. He shot one, possibly the dead man we found. There might be others around."

Mills nodded, "Yes. They carried away their dead, so to leave no evidence of their presence. Then, set the place on fire, hoping to hide their crimes."

"Except, the house is of solid brick," the deputy said. "Only the interior walls and floor burned. It was caught, and put out in time, before the bodies burned away."

"I want these monsters found!" Mills declared emphatically. "I want them on the gallows!"

MARTIN LAY in the hospital bed, staring blankly at the ceiling. Sunlight streamed through the windows, filling the ward where he lay with light, but his world was black as night. He had failed them. He had failed to protect those he loved the most. He had promised to protect them, and he had failed. Yes, he was outnumbered, but that was no excuse, his beloved Odette was dead. His girls . . . tears began to flow out of his eyes. He thought of Clarice giving him the sugar bun, and broke down in wracking sobs.

He had cried himself out the same time a doctor stopped beside his bed. "How much pain are you feeling, Mr. Ouimette?" he asked.

Martin turned his red, watery eyes to look at him, "My heart is broken. So much pain, I cannot bear it."

"Yes," the doctor said in a sympathetic voice. "I am very sorry for your loss. I do need to know, though, how much pain your body feels?"

"My head and face hurt. My chest hurts."

"You were hit numerous times in the head, causing a severe concussion. There are several cuts on your face, and broken teeth. You were unconscious when they brought you in. A dentist removed the broken teeth while you were unconscious. You also have severely bruised ribs. You were quite badly beaten."

Martin moved his tongue around his teeth to find cloth tucked into his gums in places where three teeth had once been. "Am I burned?"

"No, surprisingly. The men must have gotten you out before you burned."

"How did my wife and children die?"

"I do not know that. The sheriff, or undertaker, would be able to tell you."

"When can I leave?"

"Tomorrow, we can release you. Would you like something to help you sleep for now?"

"Yes. Then, I do not have to remember my failure." He focused his eyes on the ceiling, "Can you give me something to make me sleep forever?"

"If you are referring to suicide, no. I am sworn to protect life, not take it. If you think you can sleep your life away, there is liquor, but it is a poor choice for a man, and a cowardly way to hide from the world."

Martin looked at him, "What do you know of my world? My choices?"

"I fought in the war in eighteen-twelve, and thirteen. I came home to find my wife and children had died of smallpox. The house had been burned down to prevent its spread; I was never told." He pulled up his pants leg to reveal a wooden leg, "I lost this to a cannon ball. I know a great deal about pain, and loss, Mr. Ouimette. I also know that climbing into a bottle, contemplating suicide, or spending the rest of your life in self-pity, is no way for a man to act – *if* you are a man."

Martin held his eyes on him, "I apologize for my outburst."

"I understand your pain, and grief. Do not let it get the better of you. I will send a nurse to give you something for sleep."

"No. Let me stay awake. I need to think."

The doctor nodded, "Very well." He limped away, the wooden leg making a rhythmic thump on the floor.

He returned his attention to the white ceiling as he poured through his thoughts. He realized that he had no idea how Odette and the girls had died. Did they die from the fire, or were they murdered? He had to know. He vaguely recalled talking to Sheriff Mills, who he knew. Mills would tell him what happened.

The presence of a person standing by the bed broke his attention off the ceiling. He turned his eyes to see Prisque looking down on him. "Hello, my friend. I will not ask how you are doing, for no one could being doing well under these circumstances."

Prisque pulled over a chair and sat beside him. "I came this morning to bring your money. I was shocked to find your house burned. I asked those in the area what had happened, and I was told the house caught on fire, and you had been taken to this hospital."

"Did you hear about Odette, and my children?" Martin's lips began to quiver as he fought back the tears.

"I was told they died in the fire. Martin, I am so broken-hearted. I loved Odette, and the children. What happened?"

"It was the gang. They broke in. I shot the first one, then fought with my knife, but they swept over me and beat me into unconsciousness. I woke up outside. I had been carried out, they thought I was dead."

"Did *they* kill Odette, and the children?"

"I do not know. I will learn that when I speak to Sheriff Mills."

"I cannot believe it," Prisque said in a low voice. He sat beside Martin as they shared the silence. After a full minute, Prisque said, "I have your money with me. Do you wish to have it now?"

"No. You can have it. I have nothing left to live for, I do not need money."

"You will think differently later. I will hold it for you," Prisque answered, then he stood up. "I will leave you to your thoughts."

Martin turned his eyes back to him, "Thank you for coming." He stared at Prisque's face; he had not noticed it earlier. His right eye was swollen and bruised, and there were deep scratches down the left side of his face. "What happened to your face?"

Prisque touched the wounds, "Oh, it is a bit embarrassing. We did so well at the auction, that I stopped at the tavern to have a celebration drink. You know how it goes, I got to talking with friends, one drink led to two, then to three. I dozed off in my chair; I woke up feeling something digging into my coat pocket. I opened my eyes, the men who had been at the table with me were gone, but a tavern wench had her hand in my coat pocket trying to pick my purse. I jumped in my chair and grabbed her arm, she began to flail me with her free hand. Punching me in the face, and scratching me. I let go of her arm, and she ran out."

"That is terrible. That is why I never go to the taverns. You must put something on those cuts before they become ulcerous."

"Yes, I'll do that. I will stay in St. Charles for a few days. I want to make some inquiries as to this foul business. I will check on you again, and see if you need help."

"Thank you. I am sure in a few days, I will feel differently, but right now, I am heart-sick."

"I understand." Prisque gripped Martin's hand, "We will get through this." Releasing Martin's hand, he turned and left the ward.

THE NEXT MORNING, Martin left the hospital. He caught a carriage to take him back to the house. Getting off the carriage, he paid the driver with the money left in his pockets. As the carriage pulled away, he stood in the street staring up at the second floor. Black scorching showed on the brick outside the windows. The curtains were burned off, and the window frames blackened.

He pushed open the door to the fur room. Debris had fallen through the burned floor onto the first floor, but this floor had not been burned. He went into his office; it had been ransacked. He found the iron money box on the floor, the lock broken off. He turned it upright, to see it had been cleaned out. The two knew he had gone into the office and came out with the money. He suspected red beard. He had come down here, while the rest of the gang were upstairs.

He made his way to the stairway. It didn't appear to be burned, still he cautiously put his foot down on each step, in case it was weakened. Reaching the second floor, he pushed the door open. The smell of burned wood, and fabric immediately struck him. The walls were burned to the brick. The floor charred; the rugs partially burned. The bucket brigade had put the fire out before it completely engulfed the interior, water covered the floor. Under the partially burned table he found his pistol. He picked it up and tucked it under his belt.

He reluctantly made his way into the bedroom he had shared with Odette. The fire had been more intense here, but the bucket brigade had stopped its spread. The covers on the bed were burned. He moved across the room, and opened a window. The incoming air stirred the distinctive smell of burnt whale oil.

Scowling at the smell, he looked around the room. Running his fingers down the wall, he brought them back with a film of oil on them. He checked the badly burned bed, the remnants of the mattress and blankets were slick with oil. As he walked, almost in a daze, his foot struck something that slid across the floor. He looked down to see the pistol Odette had with her. He picked it up, it had been fired. He hoped the shot had been fatal. He kept the pistol in his hand.

He left the room and went into the girls' room. It too was more burned than the rest of the house. Oil was on the walls, and beds as well. The imagery of their last minutes of life cut into his dulled mind. He let out a cry of despair at the loss of his beloved children, and the horror no child should ever experience.

He was standing in the bedroom when he heard someone enter from the outside. He stepped out to see Sheriff Mills. Mills stiffened, momentarily startled. "Mr. Ouimette, I did not expect to find you here."

"I came to see what was left."

"I am here to look over the crime scene. What have you discovered?" Mills asked.

"The fire was deliberately set," Martin said. "The walls and beds are slick with whale oil. The bedrooms are burned far more than the living areas."

"Yes, that makes sense," Mills replied. "They wanted to burn the house down to hide their crimes. Fortunately, whale oil does not burn quickly. The proof of their crimes remains."

"Fortunately, yes," Martin answered. "I recall telling you about the gang. Have you found them?"

"No, however, we are looking for them. We did find one man dead, a street over from here. He had been shot in the chest."

"The first man through the door, I shot in the chest." Martin furrowed his brow as the sheriff's words sunk in, "You said, 'to hide their crimes'. What crimes did you find?"

"Are you sure, you want to know?"

"I want to know the truth."

Mills hesitated, trying to find the best way to tell him. "All three were murdered."

"That is apparent from the deliberate fire, but how?"

"Their throats were cut."

Martin opened his mouth, and let out a breath. He fought back a cry, then asked in a small voice, "The girls, too?"

"Yes," Mills answered softly.

Martin rubbed his hands over his face. "Oh, my babies," he moaned.

"We will find these wretches, and swing them from the gallows," Mills said with intensity. "I promise you that."

Martin took his hands down, drew in a deep breath, and let it out. "I must know one more thing. Were they molested?"

Mills hesitated.

"Your hesitation answers my question. Even the children?"

Mills hung his head and nodded.

Martin turned, rushing to a corner where he violently vomited. He stood in the corner, his head against the wall, and wept.

"They are at the undertakers whenever you are ready to make the funeral arrangements," Mills said softly.

Martin didn't answer.

Mills turned and left the room. He had learned all he needed to know. They would leave no stone unturned in finding these men.

MARTIN HAD no idea how long he had stood in the corner. He wiped his face, and went back down the stairs to the fur floor. He sat on the floor, laid Odette's pistol beside him, pulled his knees up, wrapped his arms around them, and buried his head against them. He let the tears flow.

How long he had sat like that, he didn't know, but the door opening, and soft steps approaching, caused him to look up. The room was dim, the only light coming in from the windows. His eyes were blurred from the tears, but he could make out that it was Prisque.

Prisque hunkered down in front of him. "What did you learn?"

Martin looked at him, "They molested Odette, and the girls, then cut their throats. Then, tried to burn the house to hide their crimes."

Prisque closed his eyes tightly, and winced, "How horrible. Poor, poor children."

Martin buried his face in his knees and wept.

Prisque took a deep breath, the released it. "I have been

making inquiries," he began. "A gang of men, led by a man with red beard and hair, were seen at the river docks. They were trying to find passage on a flatboat headed upriver, but there were none setting off. They walked on by foot, following the river upstream.

"I rode on to Cote Sans Dessein, and learned that ten horses had been stolen from a livery stable during the night. I talked to the man who owned the stable, and asked if he had seen the gang. He had not, however, when he checked the horses in the morning, he found ten stalls empty, and an equal number of saddles and bridles missing. They had been stolen. Beyond, Cote Sans Dessein, I talked to two old men who had been fishing, they saw ten mounted men riding west, just after dawn. They assumed they were going into the wilderness."

"I killed one, that means there were eleven, but they are gone, now," Martin said, his face still pressed to his knees.

Prisque gave Martin an intense look, "Only if you want them to be."

Martin paused a moment, then lifted his head, and looked at Prisque, "What do you mean?"

"I mean. I loved Odette as my own sister, and the girls as my own. I am not married, nor do I have children, but if such men had violated, and murdered my wife and daughters, I would hunt them to the gates of hell, and kill them all."

Martin stared at him. He had been so lost in his misery,

that retribution had not entered his mind. He had been a fighter once, skilled in weapons. Would the old Martin Ouimette have just sat in sorrow, or would he have sought his own justice?"

"What do you want to do?" Prisque asked him. "Kill them, or let them live, knowing what they did?"

"They went to the Rocky Mountains?" Martin asked.

"That's what the old men thought. It would be a good place for such men to hide, and rob, and murder."

"I do not know that country," Martin said, "I would not know where to start."

"In my inquiries, I learned of a man who does. He is living in old Fort Osage."

Martin narrowed his eyes, "Fort Osage has been abandoned for years. Why would he live there?"

"Maybe he is a man who wishes to be left alone."

"If he wishes to be left alone, why would he want to help me?"

Prisque shrugged, "You won't know until you talk to him."

"What is his name?"

"Travis Walker. The men I talked to said no one knows the beaver country better that Travis Walker."

Martin sat in silence for a long moment, before saying, "I will need to get outfitted. Did you bring my horse back with you."

"Yes, they are both in the stable. It's a good thing we

made out well at the auction. We can get outfitted for the Rocky Mountains."

Martin looked into Prisque's eyes, "We?"

"We. I am going to help you hunt down these men. That's what a friend is for." Spotting the pistol on the floor, he picked it up. The wood frame was lightly burned. "Is this yours?"

"It was Odette's. It has been fired."

Prisque stood up, and reached his hand down to Martin.

Martin grasped his hand, and Prisque pulled him up to his feet. Martin looked at him, "We will have two good riding horses."

"My horse will be good pack horse," Prisque added.

Martin drew in a deep breath, then let it out. "I must tend to the funerals first."

"Yes. That comes first," Prisque agreed. He then handed the pistol to Martin. "Kill them with this – for Odette."

A look of intensity filled Martin's whole face as he took the pistol. He held it up in his hand, and looked at it. "We will hunt these murderers to the gates of hell, and I swear, I will kill them all."

5

The three graves lay open, the caskets resting to the side of each one. Several men and women who were friends, stood around them in a solemn state. The priest opened his prayer book and read: *"In your hands, Oh Lord, we humbly entrust our sisters. In this life you embraced them with your tender love; deliver them now from every evil and bid them eternal rest. The old order has passed away: welcome them into paradise, where there will be no sorrow, no weeping, no pain, but fullness of peace and joy with your Son and the Holy Spirit forever and ever. Amen."*

The grave diggers reverently lowered the caskets into the ground, one at a time. The mourners began to drift away. Women wiping the tears from their eyes, the men leaning their heads together to exchange comments concerning the murders.

Martin stood, stunned, as tears ran down his face. Prisque stood beside him, his eyes focused on the coffins. The hollow thumps of the dirt striking the wooden caskets echoed until the dirt covered them, and only the soft sounds of dirt on dirt remained.

Martin had arranged for granite headstones to be made, and put in place. He knew he would not be there to see them erected; he would be hunting the murderers. The drive for retribution had dug deep into his brain. These men would not escape his wrath. The terror his wife and children experienced, would be heaped on them a hundred times over.

The priest stepped up beside Martin, "I am sorry, Martin. Odette, and the children, were so wonderful. It is such a horrifying thing that happened to them."

Martin looked at him, "Then, Father, you heard what the men did to them?"

"Yes. I heard. Horrible, simply horrible. The sheriff will catch them, and they will be hung for their crimes."

"He will not catch them," Martin said.

"We must have faith, Martin, that the law will prevail," the priest replied.

"It is not a matter of the law, Father. The men have fled into the wilderness, to the Rocky Mountains."

"You know this to be true?"

"Yes."

"Then, they have escaped."

"No, they have not," Martin replied firmly.

The priest looked into Martin's face. His eyes revealing that he already knew the answer. "How will they be caught, then?"

"They will be found, and they will pay. Pay dearly."

"Are *you* going to go after them?" the priest asked.

"Yes, I am. I will hunt them down like the mad dogs they are, and I will kill them."

"We are forbidden to kill, Martin," the priest said in a warning tone. "The Good God will judge them."

"Yes, Father, God will most certainly judge them – after I have killed them."

"That is a great sin, Martin. You mustn't say such things. Leave them to God. It is wrong to do as you are thinking."

Martin gave the priest a steady look, "Father, I understand why you are saying that. You would be a poor priest if you did not. Now, you must see this from my eyes. Is it wrong to exact retribution on men who violate, and cut the throat, of a thirteen-year-old child, and a sixteen-year-old girl? I should let them go unpunished for their unspeakable crimes?"

The priest stood looking at him, but let him finish.

"No, I will not! I will let it go, *when* they are all slain at my hand." He turned and walked across the cemetery grounds. Prisque fell in step with him.

"They have enough lead on us," Martin said. "We buy our outfits today, and leave tomorrow. We will ask along the way to see if anyone has seen them, but it is to Fort Osage I am bound."

Prisque nodded, "I am with you all the way. They must all die."

As they walked, Martin said to Prisque, "Thank you."

"For what?"

"For waking me up. If not for you I would still be sitting on the floor lost in my misery. Weak, and cowardly, weeping instead of fighting. The man I am, and more so, the man I used to be, is now in charge. I swear that I will not stop until I have killed the last dog of that gang."

Prisque nodded, "I couldn't see you forever sitting and weeping. Especially, when the men who murdered your family get farther away. It is necessary to mourn, but it is better to take action after you have."

They reached the street beside the cemetery. Here carriages and buggies waited, or were being driven away. The two Canada Horses, Martin and Prisque had ridden, were tied at the fence. Martin checked the cinch on his saddle as several of his friends stopped to give him their condolences, and remark about the tragedy. He nodded to each, and thanked them for attending, and for their kind words.

"What will you do now?" one man asked him. "Rebuild the house, and continue to trade in furs?"

Martin shook his head, "No. I will not be returning there."

"Where will you go?"

"Prisque and I are going to the Rocky Mountains," Martin replied.

"Going out there to hunt?"

Martin tightened the cinch, then said, without looking at the man, "I am going to hunt, yes. Hunt the men who did this, and kill them." He untied the horse, gathered the reins, and mounted.

The man looked up at him, and extended his hand, "Good hunting. I would do the same."

Martin shook his hand, "I am a very good hunter." He moved the horse out onto the street with Prisque beside him.

The rest of the day Martin and Prisque purchased the supplies they would need. Prisque had moved his horse to Martin's stable where they staged everything to pack. On the floor were sacks of dry goods, coffee, blankets, extra clothes, knives, enough powder, rifle balls, and caps to last for months. They had traded their old Long Rifles for four of the new .56 caliber Plains Rifles made by the Hawken brothers. Martin had his pistols. Prisque carried one.

Prisque dropped a dozen traps, and a roll of leather thongs, down beside the supplies.

Martin looked at the traps, "We are hunting men, not beaver."

"We may be a long time in the mountains tracking these men down. The winter snows are deep there, and we might have to wait out the winter. We will need to trap, if we are. Our money will not be good at the rendezvous, we will need pelts to trade for supplies."

Martin pondered on what Prisque had said, then nodded, "You are far-sighted, more so than me. I am thinking of a short hunt, but you are taking into account, what to do if it is not."

"It is a big land out there; from all I have been told. It will not be easy to find these men, but we will. They will be seen by other men, and they will tell us, and we will follow their trail one tale at a time."

"You are practical, and you will keep me going in a straight line, when I want to wander around like a puppy."

"We both have skills to lend. Between us, even if it takes two years, we will find them."

"I have nothing to come back to," Martin said. "I can stay out there as long as it takes."

"I'd rather be in the woods, anyway, than the city," Prisque said. "I was getting tired of it, and looking back more and more to the woods."

Martin nodded, "I have to admit, I have been as well. Odette saw the longing in my eyes. She knew I wanted back out in the woods."

"Maybe, after we kill these scoundrels, we will remain in the mountains," Prisque remarked.

"Yes, maybe. We will not have to buy traps if we do."

Prisque grinned, "I'm far-sighted – remember?"

Martin nodded, "Yes. Saddle our horses, pack the horse, and get on our way."

"I will pack the horse," Prisque said. "He is used to my hand, and a little uncooperative with others."

While Prisque packed the horse, Martin saddled the Canada Horses. Mounting, Prisque took the lead rope to the pack horse, and began to ride. Martin looked up at the house. Never again would he hear his girls laugh, look into his wife's brown eyes, or sit at the table as a family. He shook the growing pain out of his head and heart. Those men would pay, oh, how they would pay.

THE FIRST PLACE they stopped was the livery stable in Cote Sans Dessein, where the horses had been stolen. The hostler, Roger Stein, remembered Prisque. "You look like you're bound for a trip," Stein remarked.

Prisque nodded, "We are going into the Rocky Mountains in pursuit of the men I asked you about the other day."

"I have been thinking about what you told me," Stein said. "You had said, eight or ten men, scoundrels and murderers they were. Considering their number, and that they are thieves, and ten horses, and tack, was stolen, it stands to reason they are the ones who did it."

"Very likely," Prisque replied.

"What did they do, that you are in pursuit of them?" Stein asked.

"They murdered my wife, and two daughters," Martin replied.

Stein gaped at him, "How terrible! I am most sorry. I wish I could tell you more, but I was away overnight at my brother's house when they struck. I found the lock broken off the door, and the horses gone. I had been robbed, and now I must repay the men who lost their horses entrusted to me."

"It is a good thing you were not here," Martin said. "They do not hesitate to murder."

"In that respect, I am fortunate, but financially, I am in trouble now. I hope you find them."

"We will," Martin replied as he moved his horse on.

"Now, we know they are mounted," Prisque said. "As I said before, we will be able to stay on their trail by what other men see."

Martin nodded, "One tale at a time."

Prisque narrowed his eyes as a thought came to him, then looked at Martin, "The sheriff found the man you shot, we know that. You said, Odette fired her pistol, and you believe you cut some with your knife."

"That is right."

"It would seem, if they were badly wounded, they would need a doctor, but not one in St. Charles where their crimes were known."

"I know I cut deep into the arms of one after I fired my pistol, and I stabbed at others," Martin said. "Since ten horses were stolen, that would indicate no one else died and was abandoned. I agree, they would have to find a doctor, but not one in St. Charles."

"The next town west from here is Columbia, one-hundred miles on. They would have to see a doctor here, in Cote Sans Dessein, or bleed to death before reaching Columbia."

Martin held his attention on Prisque as he talked. "That makes sense, but would they stay around after stealing the horses? Surely, the owners of the horses would recognize their animals."

"Only, if they saw them. How would they know where to look?"

"True," Martin agreed. "We need to talk to all the doctors in Cote Sans Dessein."

Prisque handed the packhorse's lead rope to Martin, "Wait here." He turned the horse and rode back to the livery. Ten minutes passed before Prisque returned. "There are three doctors in this town. Two, on the main street, one on the far west side."

"If they were trying to keep the horses from being spotted, the doctor farthest out would be the best choice."

"Let's go talk to him first," Prisque said. "If he knows nothing, we will try the other ones."

They rode on through the town. To the west, the river

wound on through open fields and woods. The last building fronting the road was a neat, white house. On the gate hung a sign, 'John Hansen, Medical Physician'.

Dismounting, they tied the horses to a rail in front of the fence, opened the gate, and proceeded up the walk. Stepping up on the porch, Martin knocked on the door. A moment later, a woman opened the door. "Are you in need of the doctor?" she asked.

"No," Martin replied. "We only wish to ask him a few questions."

"Yes, come in," she said, opening the door and moving aside to let them enter.

"Thank you," Martin said, as they removed their hats upon entry.

The woman went through a door, a moment later she reappeared, a man in a suit following her. "I am Doctor Hansen; you have questions for me?"

"I will come directly to the point, doctor," Martin began. "In the past couple of days did you treat any men with gunshot, or knife wounds?"

Hansen frowned, "I am not at liberty to divulge patient information."

"Could your liberty loosen a bit if I told you these men are part of a murderous gang of robbers and cutthroats? In St. Charles, they molested a woman, and two girls, age thirteen and sixteen, then slit their throats when they were finished."

The woman put her hand over her mouth, stifling a gasp, as horror filled her eyes."

"Are these the kind of men you feel the need to protect?" Martin challenged him.

"Is this true?" Hansen asked.

"Would I say it, if it were not," Martin replied.

"Are you after these men? Are you the law?" Hansen asked.

"Yes, we are after these men. No, we are not the law. The law will never find them where they are going."

"If you are not the law . . ." Hansen began.

"Oh, for heaven's sake, John, tell them!" the woman broke in angrily. "Such fiends do not deserve to be protected. They deserve to be drawn and quartered. Tell them, or I will!"

The woman was obviously his wife. He glanced at her, then nodded his surrender. "Yes, a man with a gunshot wound to his hip, and a man with several stab wounds, and a third with severely lacerated chest and arms, were here. They told me they had been attacked by robbers, and left for dead. I treated them. I told them they should go to bed and rest, but they said they had to be going."

"Were they on horses?" Prisque asked him.

"Yes, they mounted, and rode down the road, westbound."

"Thank you, doctor," Martin said.

"Did you know the woman and children this abomination happened to?" the woman asked.

Martin looked at her, "Yes. It was my wife, and daughters."

Both the doctor, and his wife, stared at him, loose jawed, in shock. "How terrible," she said in a small voice.

"I am sorry," Hansen said. "If it helps, two were in bad shape. I am sure they will have to stop somewhere and rest. The one with the gunshot, the wound was becoming infected. He will not travel for long. You may catch them soon."

"We will catch them, alright," Martin replied. "Thank you." He and Prisque left the house.

"One tale at a time," Martin said as he stepped into the saddle.

6

They rode on until they entered the town of Columbia. Riding through it, they came to the river. Against the bank were boats, and a flatboat with men busily loading boxes and crates onto it. Other men, not associated with the flatboat, were working with their various boats.

"I wonder," Prisque began, as he looked over the activity, "will the gang stay on this side of the river, or do they need to cross over?"

"Time to ask questions," Martin replied.

Dismounting, they tied the horses to a couple of saplings, and walked down to the flatboat. A man with a sheave of papers in his hand, was comparing them to the crates waiting to be loaded on a flatboat. Martin and Prisque stood in front of him until he looked up at them.

"Has a party of eight or ten men come here looking for a boat to go upriver?" Martin asked.

"I have no idea," the man replied. "We've only been here since yesterday, getting loaded."

"Would men heading west be better off crossing the river, or staying on this side of it?" Prisque asked him.

"Depends on where they want to go," the man replied. He turned and shouted at the men loading the boat, then walked toward them.

Prisque snorted, "Well, he's helpful."

Two men, sat on barrels smoking pipes as the boat was being loaded. They were dressed in buckskin shirts, pants of the same tanned hide, rubbed smooth and black around the thighs, and fur hats on their heads. With their rifles standing upright between their knees, they studied Martin and Prisque. "Whaal," one of the trappers said, "there's two lines of thought to yer question."

Martin and Prisque turned to look at them. "What would those be?" Prisque asked him.

"If'n a man stays to this side of the river, first, he has to get through the Arikara, and they don't care much for intruders. If'n he gets past them, he's got the Sioux to get through, and they don't like intruders either, chances are they'd end up scalps. Then, if'n, by divine providence, he survived the Sioux, well, then he'd be up in Blackfoot country – that'd be the end of 'em."

"So, I take it, staying on this side of the river, is a bad idea," Prisque remarked.

The trapper sucked on his pipe and nodded.

"What does he get if he crosses the river?" Prisque asked.

"Now, across the river, is where you wanna be. By that route, you go due west to the Rocky Mountains. Indians are mostly Snakes, Flatheads, Crows, and a few other tribes, all of which got no problem with a white man. Friendly, they are. You can buy horses from the Snakes for a few beaver pelts, or other truck they might need."

"Then, crossing the river is the best way to go," Martin said.

"That it is," the trapper replied. He gave his pipe a few puffs, then asked, "You boys headin' west?"

"Maybe, it depends," Martin replied.

"On those men you're followin'?" the trapper remarked.

Martin looked in the trapper's hair-covered face, "You have seen them?"

The trapper poked in his pipe bowl with a wood splinter, then took a few hard draws on the pipe with no smoke, "Darn thing, harder to keep lit than a fire in a down-pourin' rain." He tapped it on the barrel, sucked on it, and blew out smoke, he smiled with satisfaction. "Thar, she goes. Yesterday, ten mounted men rode to Peterson's ferry," he pointed up river with the stem of his pipe, "up yonder. Mighty motley lookin' crew, they was."

Martin and Prisque looked upriver where the trapper had indicated. "We'll go talk to him," Prisque said.

"They didn't look like men fit for the mountains," the second trapper spoke up. "More like river pirates, than trappers. They'd be dead inside of a week, except they picked themselves up a pilot."

The first trapper snorted his disdain, "Luther Monk. He fits right in with that bunch."

"What can you tell us about Luther Monk?" Martin asked.

"Fur thief, trap robber, braggart, general scoundrel," the second trapper replied. "Sell his own mother to the Indians for a muskrat pelt. Kill a man for his pack."

"Does he know that country?" Prisque asked.

"He knows it enough," the trapper answered.

Martin frowned, "That puts us at a disadvantage."

The first trapper studied Martin, "You look Indian, what's your tribe?"

Martin looked at him, "Cree. I am Metis."

"So, you're a woodsman, but not a mountain man."

"I know my way around in the woods," Martin replied.

"But, not the Rocky Mountain country," the second trapper remarked. "It's a whole different animal."

Martin nodded his agreement, "I know."

"What did these men do, if you don't mind my askin', that's got yuh huntin' 'em?" the first trapper asked.

Martin met the man's calm, blue eyes, "They murdered my wife, and daughters."

"Plan to run 'em into hell, or just give it half a try?" the second trapper asked.

Martin shifted his attention to him, "They will be sent to hell when we catch them."

"Then, you'll need a pilot, to get you on their trail."

Martin nodded, "It would help. Neither of us know that country."

"You know where Fort Osage is? Across the river?"

"I have never been there, but I know of the location," Martin replied.

"There's a trail, takes up on the other side of the river, that goes right to it. It's a three-day ride. You go on up there, and you'll find a man in there, name o' Travis Walker.

Martin and Prisque exchanged glances.

"You heard of him?" the trapper asked.

"His name was given to us, yes," Martin answered.

"Well, Travis has forgot more about the beaver country, than Luther Monk ever knew."

"Problem is," the first trapper broke in, "Travis is done with the mountains. He's dug into the ruins of that old fort, and he ain't comin' out – last I heard, anyways."

"Considerin' why he's dug in there, might be a reason why he'd help these men out," the second trapper argued.

The first trapper shrugged, "Anything's possible. Don't hurt to ask him."

"Why is he in there, not wanting to come out?" Martin asked.

"Ain't for us to say," the second trapper replied. "It's Travis' business. You ask him, and he might tell you."

"First thing you want to do is head on up there to Peterson's ferry. Ask him about those men," the first trapper said.

"Thank you for your help," Martin said.

"No problem. Good luck huntin'"

"Watch your top knot," the second trapper remarked.

Martin gave him a questioning look.

"Don't get scalped," the trapper clarified.

"I'll try not to," Martin replied. He and Prisque walked toward the ferry.

The first trapper looked at his partner, "What do you think?"

"He might be green as grass for the beaver country, but that boy's been in a scrap or two. You can see it on him. I'd bet my winter's ketch; he kills the lot of 'em."

A hundred yards further up the river was Peterson's ferry. It was a steam-powered flat-bottomed ferry boat. The stack puffed out smoke as a middle-aged man, and his young son, busied themselves on the deck. Three men, and five horses, were waiting to board. Two of the horses were packed, three wore saddles. "He takes horses," Prisque said.

Approaching the boat, Martin called out, "Are you, Mr. Peterson?"

The man turned his attention to Martin and Prisque. "That's me. Room for two more if you're crossing the river."

"Not right now, maybe later," Martin replied. "What we want to know is whether you took a party of eleven mounted men across the river in the past few days?"

"I take a lot of men and horses across the river; can you describe them better?"

"They are a crew of cutthroat scoundrels, . . ." Martin began.

Peterson chuckled, "Most of the men going into the beaver country are scoundrels."

"Very likely," Martin agreed. "They are led by a Scotsman, red beard, long red hair. It is possible there are others who are Scots, or Englishmen. If they spoke you would hear the accents."

"Yes, there was a Scotsman with red beard and hair, and there *were* eleven of them, all tolled. I had to take them over in two loads because this boat won't carry that many at once. One was a man who I took to be their guide. He had the look of a beaver man to him."

"Were two of them acting injured?" Martin asked. "Limping, showing signs of being slowed down?"

"Yes. One was limping badly, and groaning when he did. Another had trouble lifting his arms."

"That would be them," Martin said.

"I took them across. There's a trail on the other side that

goes past old Fort Osage, and on toward the mountains. They took off on it."

"Did you hear any of their conversation?" Prisque asked.

"They didn't talk much, but I did hear one of them call red-beard, Duncan."

"The name resonated in Martin's mind. The face and name suddenly joined. He did know him. Several years had passed, but it was the same man, Duncan Black. He had been one of Macdonell's thugs in the Red River colony. He was also a thief, and a river pirate.

Martin gestured toward the horses waiting to load, "Can you take three more horses across?"

Peterson shook his head, "Six is the limit. When we come back, I'll take you across. Charge'll be ten dollars."

"Okay," Martin agreed. "When are you leaving?"

"As soon as we get these horses on board," Peterson replied. "Be ready when we come back."

"We will be here," Martin replied. He and Prisque walked back for their horses.

Leading the horses back to the ferry launch, they watched the steam-powered flatboat push across the strong current of the river. Its stack intensely puffing smoke, as it aimed for a point upstream from its starting point on the north bank. Pushing into the south bank, the young man dropped the loading ramp onto a flat bank that had been cleared of trees and brush. The horses and men left the boat and began riding west. The ramp was put back up in place, and the boat began to chug back across the current to the north side.

Sliding into the bank, the young man dropped the ramp. Martin and Prisque led the horses onto the flatboat, and held the reins. Martin handed Peterson a ten-dollar note. Pocketing the note, Peterson manned the controls and set off for the south bank.

"This is quite a boat you have here," Martin remarked.

Peterson nodded, "She's the only steam-powered ferry up here."

"I have seen steamboats on the Mississippi, and Missouri," Martin said. "Do they come up this far?"

Peterson shook his head, "The big steamboats were trying to see how far they could get upriver, but the farthest they could get is Council Bluff. After that, sawyers, shallow water, high water, all manner of problems wrecks them, so they quit trying. Talking to one steamboat Captain, he said their goal is to reach the Yellowstone River, but they never will. That river eats boats. My little boat is perfect for the river."

"Yes, she handles the river well," Martin remarked.

"Heading for the Rocky Mountains?" Peterson asked.

"Depends on where our quarry leads us."

"What did they do? It must have been bad for you to pursue them into the wilderness."

"They murdered my wife and two daughters," Martin replied.

"Oh. They did look like a wretched bunch of devils."

"They are," Martin replied as he stared toward the approaching bank. "If they are carrying wounded, they might have stopped at Fort Osage."

Peterson looked at Martin, "You do know that Fort Osage has been abandoned for years. The place is falling apart. No one stops there anymore."

"It is still a place to rest the wounded," Martin replied.

Peterson nodded, "I suppose."

Reaching the south bank, the young man dropped the ramp down on the flat, mud churned bank. The number of horseshoe tracks indicated that many riders had gotten off here. Martin and Prisque led the horses off the boat.

"Good luck finding your quarry," Peterson called out to them. "Just follow that trail, goes right to Fort Osage, and on past it."

Martin waved his acknowledgement back to him, then mounted his horse.

7

The trail they followed went away from the river, across open fields, and was easily traveled. It was well trod by years of horse, wagon, and foot traffic. They studied the tracks from their saddles. The five horses that had proceeded them left fresh shod tracks in the trail, but the group was out of sight. Those were on top of numerous horseshoe prints, which ones belonged to the gang was impossible to tell.

On the third day, the river was back in sight, and in the distance, they could see the standing palisade of the fort. On the corners of the square structure were two guard towers in the process of falling down. A two-story house, with stone fireplaces covering most of both side walls, rose above the palisade's upright logs. A thin line of smoke drifted out of one of the chimneys.

As they drew nearer, it was clear that in the eight years the fort had been abandoned, weather had taken its toll. Many of the palisade logs had fallen, leaving gaps in the once protective wall. One of the corner guard houses had fallen, the second was leaning heavily, as its supports had rotted away. The gate was lying on the ground where it had fallen.

Riding through the open gateway, they could see lines of shops, barracks, and a store along the inner wall. All abandoned, save for the anvil, and a few forgotten tools in the blacksmith shop. Horse tracks, along with piles of horse manure, were evident in the grass growing out of the ground that had once been trampled into dust. One horse was staked out on the grass, a second saddled horse, dragging reins, grazed close to it.

They stopped, and looked around. The porch roof over the upper floor's balcony had collapsed. Several of the posts holding up the porch roof on the ground floor, had broken down, leaving that portion of roof sagging to within four feet of the wooden floor surrounding three sides of the house. The door was closed, the porch over it, and several feet to either side, had new posts holding it up.

Prisque pointed at the chimney top, high above them, "There's smoke, someone is in there."

"Must be where Travis Walker is living," Martin said.

"Let's find out." Prisque dismounted, draping the lead

rope to the pack horse over the saddle. Martin dismounted as well.

"No one invited you in," came a voice from a window with the shutters open. "Get back on your horses, and keep goin'."

"And, if we don't?" Martin replied.

"I'll shoot you," returned the voice.

"I do not believe you will," Martin said.

"Don't be so sure."

"If you were that frightened of someone coming in, you would have shot us already," Martin came back.

"I'm not frightened, I don't want people comin' 'round my home."

"It is not your home," Martin said. "It was a trading fort, built by William Clark. Unless Mr. Clark gave it to you, you are a squatter."

"It's my home now, so get out!"

"No!" Martin replied tersely.

"What do you want?" the voice snapped angrily.

"I want to talk to Travis Walker."

"Travis Walker's an old yarn spun by drunken trappers. He doesn't exist. You wasted your time lookin' for a man who doesn't exist."

Martin looked at Prisque, who shrugged, "Maybe, he is just a legend."

"I doubt it," Martin replied in a low voice. "That is him." In a louder voice, Martin said, "We talked to a couple of old trappers who said Travis Walker was not much of a mountain man. That he was hiding in this old fort, because he was afraid to go back into the mountains. If you are Travis Walker, then they were right. You are afraid to even come out of that falling down shack, so, it stands to reason you are afraid of the mountains."

There was no rebut from the hidden man.

Catching on to Martin's attempt to force Walker out, Prisque added, "They said Luther Monk was a better trapper. Then, again, if Travis Walker is just a story, then Luther Monk would be the better mountain man. I guess you aren't Travis Walker after all."

"Luther Monk is sack of mule marbles!" shot back the voice. "Always was, always will be, until his scalp is hangin' off some Blackfoot devil's coup stick, or mine."

"Why should it matter to you, if you never return to the mountains," Martin said. "Let Luther Monk be the man they tell stories about, instead of Travis Walker – who does not exist."

The door opened, creating an entry less than six feet high. A man appeared in it; he had to duck down to pass through the door. Straightening to his full height, his head was several inches above the top of the door. His brown eyes glowered at Martin from above a full beard. "You are an annoying little mosquito. Still, you have some nerve, for a runt."

Martin, who feared no man, regardless of his size, met

his eyes, "Mosquitos *are* very annoying. They can also drive a great bear to run wild, and jump into a lake in fear of them."

The man's eyes lightened, then he burst out with a roaring laugh. "By thunder, you are a nervy little runt! I'd kill you for your insults, but I have to admire your tenacity. You remind me of an ermine, take on something ten times its size, and think he can win."

"My father used to say, that it did not matter how big, or tall, a man was. It was what was inside him that made him a giant, or a mouse – or runt, as you put it."

The man leaned his shoulder against one of the new porch posts, and nodded, "Your pa was right." He shifted his eyes to Prisque, "How about you? Got anything to say?"

Prisque shrugged, "If I do, you'll hear it."

The big man laughed, "Another mosquito. I can tell by your talk, you're a Frenchman." He looked back at Martin, "I'm not sure what you are. You look Indian, but not altogether, and it's a tribe I've not seen."

"I am Metis. My father is a trapper from the Lake Winnipeg country, and my mother is Cree."

The man nodded, "I've heard of Metis. They are a nervy breed of woodsmen. Okay, what do you want?"

"Are you Travis Walker?" Martin asked.

"Yeah. What do you want with him?"

"I want his help."

"I don't help people. I mind my own business, and

expect people to mind theirs. You've interfered with my life, and I've given you the courtesy of listening, and not killing you. So, you can go now."

"You have no life," Martin said abruptly. "You hide in this falling down fort. Why you do, is your own business, but do not tell me it is your life. Life is lived, not buried in a rotting building."

Travis held his eyes on Martin, "You speak your mind, don't you?"

"I say what needs to be said."

Travis' eyes held a lock on Martin's eyes. Martin held the lock, without wavering, or turning his eyes away.

Travis was beginning to like the little woodsman. He admired a man with nerve, and had no use for weaklings, cowards, or braggarts. "Why do you want my help?"

"We need you to guide us through the beaver country."

"If you're fixin' to be mountain men, then you need to figure it out for yourself, like we all had to. Don't expect me to give you a shortcut by my tellin' you how to do everything. Trap your own beaver, fight the Indians yourselves. I ain't goin' back out there to nursemaid a couple of greenhorns."

Martin held his lock on Travis' eyes. He felt his temper begin to rise, but fought it back down. Shouting in anger would not help his cause. "We are not interested in being mountain men, or trapping beaver. I have fought men; I have no fear of a fight."

Travis frowned at him, trying to figure the little Metis out. "You are a complicated little mosquito. You don't want to trap beaver, so why go into the country? Why don't you just get to the point of the matter?"

"We are hunting a gang of murderers. They escaped into this country. We do not know the country, and need a guide to help us."

Travis scratched his head of shaggy brown hair, "Well, that's one I haven't heard before. Why are you huntin' 'em?"

"They broke into my house, molested, and murdered my wife, and daughters. I was there, I shot one, and used my knife on the others. My wife shot, and wounded one. I was beaten senseless to the floor, and left for dead. We have followed them since St. Charles, where it happened. We learned that they crossed the river on the ferry below Columbia, and headed this way."

Travis stared at him, without comment, for a long minute. Then, he asked, "How old were your daughters?"

"Sixteen, and thirteen. Just children. When the gang finished, they cut their throats."

"How bad do you want to find 'em?" Travis asked.

"Bad enough to ask you for help."

"I mean, how far are you willin' to go, and through what, to find 'em?"

"Is hell, too far?" Martin replied succinctly.

"You figure to kill 'em?"

Martin drew in a breath, stretching to his full five-seven, "Every one of them. None will escape, if I have to spend the rest of my life hunting them."

"You get up into some of that country, especially among the Blackfeet, and it just might be the rest of your life – very quickly."

"If you are trying to frighten me, your words hold no value with me."

Travis continued to look at Martin, "You seem determined to see it through. What if I say, I'm not interested in helpin' you?"

"Then, we will ride on, and figure it out for ourselves."

Travis looked at Prisque, "You, the quiet one, with the squaw claws on your face, what's your stake in this?"

Prisque frowned at him, "Squaw claws?"

Travis gestured at Prisque's face, "Those scabbed over scratches on your face, I've seen that on trappers who got too amorous with squaws, and they raked their faces with their claws. She must have been pretty mad."

"It isn't what you're thinking," Prisque remarked brusquely.

"A tavern wench tried to pick his pocket, when he stopped her, she raked him," Martin said in defense of his friend.

Travis looked Prisque's face over, "Really."

"Yes, *really!*" Prisque shot back. "I had too much to drink. I dozed off at the table. I woke up with a woman's right hand in my inside coat pocket. I grabbed her arm, and she beat and scratched my face."

Travis continued to study Prisque's face, "Hmm, interestin'."

"I don't care for your implication that I was having a tryst with a woman of ill-repute," Prisque snapped. "Martin is my friend. I was close to his family. I'll go wherever the chase takes us. Does that answer your question!"

"A true friend, huh?"

"Yes," Prisque replied.

"True friends are a rare commodity," Travis said. "Them that stick with you through thick and thin are few and far between. You got a name?"

"Prisque Tremblay."

"Are you from up north, too?"

"My family is from Canada, north of Lake Ontario. We were all trappers – Couriers."

"What's a *Courier*?" Travis asked.

"Free trappers. We refused to purchase the licenses the British expected us to buy in order to trap. We were considered outlaws, because we trapped as free men."

Travis nodded, "Being a free man is worth fightin' for." He turned his attention back to Martin. "Where do you come from?"

"The Red River country. I worked for the Northwest Fur Company."

"How did you end up down here?"

"That would be my business. Why are *you* hiding here, instead of being out in the mountains?" Martin came back.

"Maybe, when I get to know you better, I'll tell you."

"That is my answer as well."

"Fair enough," Travis replied. "Tell me about this gang."

"Two men at the river, where we took the ferry, saw them," Martin began. "They said, there were ten. They are led by a Scotsman named Duncan Black, but they hired Luther Monk to guide them."

Travis gave a slight nod, "Monk is scum on his best days. An outlaw, thief, and killer. If he's guidin' them, they plan to steal and murder."

"Did they pass this way?" Martin asked.

"Fact is, they did ride into here. They planned on stayin' a while. Me and Luther Monk are old enemies. I caught him takin' a beaver from one of my traps. He took a rifle ball in the back for his trouble. He lived through it, but he's plum scared of me. When I saw that pack of wolves ride in here, I told 'em to ride out. They needed some persuadin', but they did, all but one."

"What happened to the one?" Martin asked.

"Seems he was badly injured. He couldn't keep up, so they threw him off here." Travis pointed at the row of dilapidated barracks, "He crawled into that one right there. He ain't come out, might be dead in there, 'cause his horse is still here."

Martin turned to look at the place Travis had pointed

out. He went to his horse, and took Odette's pistol with the scorched stock, out of the saddlebag. He began walking toward the barrack. Prisque fell in behind him. Travis followed them, curious to see what the little Metis was going to do.

Reaching the barrack, Martin pushed open the door. A shaft of sunlight illuminated the room, as did an unshuttered window. Lying on a rotting straw mattress on a woodframed bed was the Frenchman who had been with Duncan the day they sold him the furs. He had shown too much interest in Odette when she inadvertently appeared that day.

The man looked at Martin, clearly recognizing him, his eyes growing wide with fear. He sat up on the bed, pressing himself hard against the wall, as if to disappear into it. He stared at Martin; his face glistening with sweat, even though it was a cool day.

Martin glowered at him, "You have a pistol ball in your hip, no?"

"Yes. I was attacked by robbers."

"Liar," Martin said calmly. "You were with Duncan Black in my fur house."

The man showed alarm at the mention of Duncan's name, and that Martin knew who he was.

"Oh, yes, I know who you both are. You and your miserable scum, broke into my house, and murdered my family."

"That wasn't me," the man sputtered out. "I had no part

in that. That was all Duncan's idea. I told him to leave the women alone, but he wanted the women. I argued with him, and refused to go in."

"They were not *women*, they were *children!*" Martin shouted at him. "You were the first one in my wife's room. You went in to attack her, but she fired a pistol ball into you. That is how you were shot. You were not attacked by robbers; you were shot trying to rape an innocent woman."

"No, that's not true," the man cried out in near panic. "I wasn't there."

"I will hunt you all down, and you will all die at my hand." Martin cocked the pistol, and pointed it at the man's forehead. The man began to plead for mercy, but his cry was covered by the exploding shot. His head jerked back, thumping hard against the wall, his lifeless body sliding sideways down to the bed.

Martin turned his head to see Travis watching him. Prisque stepped in behind him. "Now, there are only nine to find," Martin said.

Travis looked at the dead man, and then studied Martin for a moment. "You'll do to take along. Go tend to your horses. I've got a venison stew cooking; we'll parley some more about hunting down these child killers. I might be interested." He turned and left the room.

8

Travis sat up late into the night, smoking his pipe, and staring into the flames licking at the slow-burning oak in the fireplace. He considered Martin's situation. He and Prisque had long since went into a barrack to sleep. Martin had guts, and a sense of mountain man justice. No man, worth a lick of salt, would let a gang of cutthroats do what they did to his wife and children, and not hunt them down. The little Metis had not hesitated to finish off that man in the barrack. That proved his nerve, and resolve.

The image of a young brown-haired woman of French blood, and two girls, ten and twelve years of age, came vividly to mind. The image was painful, yet locked permanently in his minds-eye, and wanted it to be so. It was the other image, of two stalwart twin boys, that held sway over his life. He had proven his resolve then, just like the little Metis was proving his now, but then he had crawled into a hole, and pulled the hole in after him. How long had he been in this hole? Two years? Yes, two and a half years ago he had led them down to the Medicine Bow mountains. A mistake he had lived to regret.

It was ten years ago, 1822, when they struck out for the wilderness with a loaded pack horse. Over the next eight years they had followed every stream, crossed every pass, and circled every lake between the Platte, and the Yellowstone. They traded with the friendly Indians, and fought, or escaped by the skin of their teeth, every hostile tribe in the country. It was in '24, when they were at Fort Atkinson, selling beaver pelts, and resupplying, that he encountered William Ashley, and his brigade of trappers.

Ashley was impressed at the fact they had been so long in the mountains, and still alive. He was also interested in the large number of beaver pelts they had collected. Ashley asked them to join his brigade. They refused, having no interest in working for anyone, but they did find their way to Ashley's rendezvous on Henry's Fork. It was a small affair, compared to those that followed.

It was the 1830 rendezvous on the Wind River, when the talk was about the beaver to be had down south of the North Fork of the Platte. The streams of the Medicine Bow mountains, across the Laramie plains, were lightly trapped. It was Cheyenne country, but they were children compared to the wretched Blackfeet they had been surviving for years. It was his decision to head down to the Medicine Bow country.

He clasped his hands over his face, *God-in-Heaven,* how he wished he never heard of that country. That he had been away that day when the trappers talked about it, how . . .. He shook his head; he was trekking back over old trails best left in the past, but should they be left behind?

He took his hands down from his face, and stared wearily into the flames. Was it better to let the bad memories run out the good ones? To abandon good memories of the past, so bad ones could haunt him day and night? To destroy his sleep with bloody nightmares? What was to be gained by letting himself rot away, hidden from the world in a falling down fort? When it finally fell to the ground, what would he do. Go find another hole to crawl into?

Maybe, he needed something like Martin to bring him out of his hibernation. They had talked further about what happened at his house. The man needed to make the brutal murderers of his family pay the ultimate price. He would wander the country forever, looking, but never finding them. Luther Monk knew the country well enough to stay ahead of Martin, while they continued in their criminal ways.

He stared into the fire, his conscience beating him like a stubborn mule, until he saw his own face looking back at him. "Coward!" the face said aloud. He stared harder; he was imagining things; he had been awake too long. The Indians ate things that made them see visions, but he had not eaten anything except venison, or was the man inside him, taking shape because he was too stubborn to listen to the voice. Coward? Maybe he was a coward. Hiding in this wreck, afraid to face the world again.

"The man needs your help," the face spoke again. Travis stared at it; the voice was distinct. "He came to you for help, and you are too full of self-pity and cowardice to help him. You, of all people, should understand his heartache, and drive for justice. You can find those men, but that's fine, you just sit in your rotting house, and pretend you're living. The men who knew the fierce reputation of Big Walker, who hunted, trapped, and drank with him at rendezvous, would spit at his feet in disgust at the coward he has become."

Travis wiped his hands over his face, and looked back in the fire. All he saw was blackened wood, and flames. "That was unsettling," he whispered to himself. Unsettling, yet there was a heap of truth to it. He had become a shell of the man he had once been. Now, was the time of decision, rot here forever, filled with self-pity, guts run out like a slit-open buffalo, or get back into the mountains, and help Martin. He heard the final challenge, loud and clear, "Get on with living, or just take the cowards way, and blow your brains out. Make a decision, man!"

. . .

AT FIRST LIGHT, Travis was in the yard walking up to his blue roan with a halter. The horse was one of the Nez Perce war horses, they called Palouse horses. The stud was big boned, muscled, and could run fast and hard, a trait that once saved him from a war party of Blackfeet up on the Musselshell.

He needed a pack horse, the bay that belonged to the dead man, had herded up with his own horse. It still bore the saddle, and trailing the reins. It was a sturdy animal, fit to pack a load. Haltering the roan, the bay followed as he led his horse to the shed that held his saddles and supplies. Tying the roan to the rail, he opened the shed door, and picked a halter off the peg. Removing the bay's bridle, he slipped the halter over its muzzle, and tied him beside the sorrel.

Going inside the shed, he began to sort through his supplies. Cooking gear, traps, tarps, tanned elk hides, axes, hatchets, and knives wrapped in elk hide. All the things he had traveled with for years, but not touched in the last two. Dust covered everything, mice had been all through it, leaving piles of their nesting litter and droppings over it all. He took a deep breath, and whispered, "Okay, old man in the fire, I've made my decision." He dragged a pack tarp out into the open and shook it out.

Piece-by-piece, he took everything out and spread it over the grass. Looking it over, he considered what he still had, and what he needed to replace. Mostly he needed food, dry goods, he had some left, but he needed more. Meat was not an issue, he could shoot, and eat, any number of animals. He needed salt, flour, coffee, beans, or rice, whichever he could get.

Martin stepped out of the barrack, and scanned the compound. His eyes stopped on Travis. "Prisque," he called back to the barrack.

Prisque walked out, "What?"

Martin pointed at Travis across the compound, "What do you make of that?"

They both looked at Travis, dressed in black wool pants, leather boots that went to his knees, a gray wool shirt, and a wide brimmed, weather-beaten hat with an eagle feather stuck through the side. His supplies spread over the ground. "I think he made a decision," Prisque remarked.

"We should find out," Martin said. They began walking across the yard.

Stopping beside Travis, Martin asked, "Going somewhere?"

"Figure we need to head up to the Platte," Travis replied. "That's where most of the trappers are startin' from, and the supply boats put in. Monk will lead that pack of coyotes to where the people are. You can't steal from others where there ain't no one to steal from. I know a lot of men back in there, they can tell me if Monk passed their way. We'll track him down."

"We'll find them, one story at a time," Martin remarked.

Travis turned his head to look at him, "That's one way of puttin' it."

Martin understood that Travis was going to help them, it didn't need to be said. He had made no commitment the night before, but somewhere during the night, he decided to help.

"We have a lot of supplies," Prisque said to Travis, "what are you short of?"

"Mostly dry goods, salt, flour, beans, coffee. I've got some inside, it'll have to do until I can reach a post."

"We have plenty of all that," Prisque said. "We'll share."

Travis nodded, "That'll work, good. Decidin' what to take. Don't know if I need the extra trap weight."

"We're bringing traps," Prisque said. "If we end up on this hunt come winter, we'll have to take a camp. We might as well trap, we'll need pelts to trade for supplies."

"Good thinkin'," Travis remarked. "When I run into some trappers, I'll ask where the rendezvous will be this year. We can get supplies there if we need 'em."

"When are the rendezvous usually?" Martin asked.

"July, most times, August at the latest. The supply trains start from St. Louis in April. By the time they reach the Rockies, and find a spot, it's summer. Why don't you go get your horse packed. We need to get out of here, that bunch has enough lead on us. We need to cut it down."

Martin and Prisque headed for their horses that were

picketed on the grass. "Something changed his mind," Martin said, "but I am far from asking what it was. I am just glad he did."

Prisque nodded his agreement, "He knows everyone in the mountains. They'll know where Monk has gone."

"Wherever he goes, that gang will be with him," Martin said. "They might think Monk is a help to them, but, our having Travis, means he will be their downfall."

WITH THEIR HORSES SADDLED, and Prisque's sorrel horse packed, they walked across the yard leading the horses. Travis was tying down the canvas covered pack over the packsaddle he had set on the bay. Protruding from a leather sheath on the outer side of his right boot was the long, black handle of a knife, the sheath at least twelve inches long. In his belt, on the left side, was its twin, on the right side a powder horn, and a leather pouch hung from leather bands over his left shoulder. Tied to the roan's saddle were two buckskin cases, one on each side, with rifle stocks protruding from them.

Travis turned to look them over as they drew closer. He saw the pistol in each of their belts, as well as the six-inch knifes most woodsmen carried. "Do you men have fightin' knives? Not meat knives, but fightin' knives."

"Not like those you are wearing, but I know how to fight with mine," Martin replied.

"Goin' into Indian country, you'll want fightin' knives. Indian attacks are often fast and close in. Too close for a gun, so that's what the knife is for. You can carve up a scalp-greedy redskin pretty quick with a good knife." He suddenly realized that Martin was half Indian. "Meanin' no offense to your blood, Martin. The Cree, Chippewa, and other Canada Indians, are pretty decent folks, peaceful, and not huntin' trouble. Indians down here are brutal, always huntin' scalps, and whatever they can steal. They'll kill a man, woman, or child, white, or Indian, they don't care. Scalp 'em, and go on thinkin' themselves something special."

Martin nodded, "I understand. I am not offended. I have heard the stories about the Indians in the Rocky Mountains. They are bad."

Travis nodded, "There are tribes friendly with the trappers, though. Death on their Indian enemies, but okay with the white man. Shoshones, or Snakes, as we call 'em are decent. The white man will find a friendly camp with them. Flatheads, the same. Crow, generally alright, I have made friends among the Crow, but they'll steal your eyeballs right out of your head, if you ain't careful. Sioux can go one way or the other, most times they'd just as soon kill you. Arapahoe, the same. Cheyenne, . . ." his face grew tense with suppressed rage, "are murdering *devils*, no better than the Blackfeet butchers."

Martin and Prisque both caught the sudden anger rise up in Travis when he mentioned the Cheyenne.

"You'll learn all of 'em, as we go along. In the meantime, we need to get you some fightin' knives."

"Those knives you are wearing, where do those come from," Martin asked. "I have never seen anything like them."

Travis pulled the knife sheathed to his boot. The blade was long, double the width of a butcher's knife. The handle was black wood, one and half times the width of his hand, but it fit fully into Travis' big hand. These are the Bowie design. Created by Rezin Bowie in Louisiana, but his brother, James, made it a fightin' knife. I once cut a Cheyenne plum in half with one swipe. I keep 'em sharp enough to cut you from five feet away." He slipped it back into the sheath.

"Will we have to wait for Rendezvous to get them?" Prisque asked.

"I have two more in my pack; you can use 'em until you get your own. When we stop tonight, I'll get 'em out, and show you how to use 'em." He looked at the rifle stocks sticking out of the leather scabbards on Martin and Prisque's saddles, "What kind of rifles you got there? From the stocks, they look like Hawkens."

"They are," Martin replied. "We each have two, the others are in the load."

"They ain't doin' you no good there. You'll need 'em on

the saddles, one on each side. You get one shot, two if you got a pistol. That second rifle might just save your life. We can make scabbards from an elk hide I have, then hang them rifles where they can do you some good."

In the few minutes they had been with Travis they had already learned more then they knew before. He had become a different man from the one they first met. He had transitioned from a man hiding from the world, to a mountain man, fully sure of himself. His experience, and knowledge, spilling out in his words, and trappings.

Tying off the pack rope, Travis turned to face Martin and Prisque. He looked over their horses, "Those are some nice horses. Keep 'em close in camp, and never take your eyes off 'em, 'cause every Indian in the country will want 'em. Especially the Crows, they're the worst horse thieves in the Rocky Mountains. I recall old Knife Creek Mike, tellin' me that he was ridin' down the Tongue River, right in the middle of Crow country. He was leadin' his pack horse, and whistlin' a tune, happy as a hummingbird in a spring flower. He said, he never heard a thing, but all of sudden he found himself sittin' on the ground, holdin' a lead rope with nothin' on the end of it. That's how fast Crow's steal your horses."

Martin grinned, "Is that a true tale?"

"Sure," Travis replied. "Mike was never known to spin a yarn," he grinned, "except on every occasion he could." Travis realized, he was looking forward to being back in the mountains, and seeing all his old friends again. He had been holed up like a wounded animal long enough.

THE FIRST DAY out they crossed the Kansas River, making their camp beside Independence Creek, a short stream that flowed into the Missouri. Near them was a village of Kickapoos. As they set up their camp, six members of the village walked up to them. Martin and Prisque watched as Travis greeted them, and they greeted him in friendly terms. They began to converse in sign language.

The exchange of hand gestures went on for several minutes, then Travis went into his packs and brought out six twists of tobacco. Handing one to each of the Indians, they smiled at their gifts, and walked away.

"What did you learn?" Martin asked Travis.

"They wanted to know our intentions on their land. I told them we were only passin' through. That we were huntin' a party a white men who murder women and children. They did see them pass by. They didn't stop, but kept headin' north toward the Platte. So, we're headin' in the right direction. Figured Monk would aim for the Platte."

"It is good to know we are on the right trail," Martin remarked.

"One tale at a time, isn't that how you said it?" Travis asked Martin.

Martin nodded his agreement. "Once they reach the Platte, where do you think they will go?"

"West, toward the Rockies. They'll try and pick off lone trappers, steal what they have. Most have their winter catches of pelts with them, waitin' for the rendezvous. Pretty rich treasure for a bunch of black-hearted pirates. I'm sure to see some men near the mouth of the Platte, flat-boats put in there droppin' off trappers headin' west, and supplies. Trappers sometimes come down to get supplies from the boats. We'll find out what they have to say about our gang."

Prisque began to build a fire, while Martin took a leather bucket to the stream. Filling it with water, he brought it back to the fire that was catching on the bone-dry cottonwood. Taking the coffee pot, he poured in water and coffee grinds, and put it on the fire. Travis walked up to them holding the two Bowie knives.

Travis handed the sheathed knives to them, "Take off those skinnin' knives, and set these on your belts."

Both men took off the shorter knives. Taking the Bowies, Martin was surprised at the weight of the heavy blade. Pulling the knife from the sheath, he was impressed to find the handle and blade balanced the knife perfectly.

"You can see by the weight," Travis began, "why this is such a handy weapon. That heavy blade, swung with a powerful arm, will cut a man in half. If you thrust with it, it'll go through bone and cartilage like a hot knife in buffalo tallow." He showed them the correct way to hold the knife for maximum effect.

"It's so perfectly balanced," Prisque remarked.

"That's right, it's a fightin' knife, and has no other use. I have smaller knives that I use for cuttin' up meat. Don't want my Bowie dulled on deer bones when I might need it in a hurry."

Prisque nodded, "I can understand that."

"You lay the blade flat, when swingin' it," Travis explained. "Swing it high for the neck, or low for the guts, from right to left, then turn your wrist over, bring it directly back, left to right. If you turn it so the blade is up, stick it in, and bring it straight up, hard. To finish a man off, stab it in his throat or heart."

Travis demonstrated some of the proper techniques for fighting in close. Martin and Prisque imitated what he showed them. Travis watched with a critical eye. Martin understood the art of knife fighting. Prisque handled the knife like a man used to skinning pelts, but it was almost like he was deliberately trying to be clumsy with it. He wondered why he was.

Travis looked back at Martin, "Who taught you to knife fight?"

"My father, he is a skilled fighter."

"Is he still up on the Red River?"

"Yes. Him and my mother. They stay with their people."

"You're more of a wanderin' nature?"

Martin shrugged, "Sometimes."

Travis studied the little Metis, he liked him more with each passing day. It was clear there was a reason he left the Red River. The Metis, from all he had heard, were a breed of home-body people. They might wander for fur, but always returned home. It takes something to force them to go so far away from their people. There was a story behind Martin that he wasn't willing to divulge, but then, there was a story behind him, that he kept to himself as well. He, and Martin, were men, despite their physical size, who were cut from the same cloth.

9

hree days from Independence Creek they reached the north fork of the Platte River where it emptied into the Missouri. As luck would have it, a flatboat was pulled into the south shore. At least a dozen trappers stood in front of the boat as the owner opened packs on the shore.

As they drew nearer, Travis began to recognize some of the men. So intent were the trappers on trading pelts for supplies, they failed to notice the three men ride up, and stop behind them. "Little early for rendezvous, ain't it?" Travis called out to the assembled men.

One buckskin clad man, grizzled beard, and hair plunging out from under a coyote skin hat, turned to look at him. He gaped at Travis for several seconds, then let out a whoop, "Whaal! Call me a pilgrim, and feed me to the Blackfeet squaws, if it ain't Big Walker!"

"Coon Eyes Charlie," Travis called back, showing a wide grin "You *are* a pilgrim!"

Coon Eyes let out a loud laugh, "Ain't it the truth!"

Several other men turned around.

"I sware, it's the ghost of Big Travis Walker, come back to wreak revenge on the whole redskin tribe!" a trapper with a deep growl for a voice croaked out.

"Bullfrog Kincaid," Travis shouted, "I ain't no ghost! Do you think there's a single redskin buck in all the Rocky Mountains can kill *me*?"

"Never figger there was, but we done heared you had gone under, gone beaver you was," Bullfrog said in a hoarse growl.

Coon Eyes walked up beside Bullfrog, "The last we heared the Cheyenne had cut you up and done et yer heart so's they'd be as brave as Kills Many Quickly. Then, you just disappeared, and no one heared no more of Big Walker. So, we figgered the story was true. Now, here yah are, bigger'n life, but still just as ugly." He let out a war whoop, "Lord A'mighty, it's fine to see you again!"

"Step on down here, yuh big pile o' bear dung, and shake hands with your old pals!" Bullfrog demanded.

Travis dismounted and exchanged rough handshakes with his friends.

"Big Walker," a man in the group hovering over the

open crates, called out, "If you need anything, best get it now, or wait half-a-lifetime for rendezvous."

Travis moved into the crowd, he slapped the man on the back, "How you been, Hugo?"

"Fine as frawgs hair. Fine as frawgs hair, Big Walker," Hugo replied as he stood up straight and shook Travis' hand.

"I see you still got your topknot," Travis said to him. "As crazy as you are for the red women, I figured some jealous husband'd have your scalp on his belt, and your skinned hide for an arrow quiver, by now."

Hugo laughed. With a wink he said, "That's only if I gets caught."

"You're goin' to one of these days, and you know it," Travis said.

Hugo grinned, showing his broken teeth, "But, I'll die a happy man. Everyone at the last rendezvous at Willer Valley said you had gone under. The Cheyenne's had kilt yuh."

Travis shook his head, "Nah. I just needed to get away for a while, but I'm back."

"Mighty sorry about the boys," Hugo said, "Mighty sorry. Everyone liked 'em."

Travis nodded, "Yeah. They paid for it."

Coon Eyes walked up and joined them. "I heared you kilt, fifty-sixty of the bloodthirsty red varmints."

"More like, forty," Travis replied.

"The whole army of trappers, and half the Crow nation, was ready to storm the red devils, and kill everyone for what they did," Hugo said. "It was ol' Short-leg who said we needed to stand back and let Big Walker take his vengeance. If need be, we'd all ride on 'em, but let you have at 'em first."

"I appreciate that," Travis said. "I did want to gut the bunch myself. How is Short-leg?"

"Gone beaver," Hugo answered. "Blackfeet caught him up on the Yellastone. Turned him over to the squaws – you know what that means," He gave a voluntary shudder, "Gives a man the crawls, and night sweats, just thinkin' about it."

Travis shook his head slowly, "Poor, Short-leg."

Hugo looked up at Martin and Prisque, "See you got yourself some new partners."

The two dismounted, and walked up to the men. Travis introduced Martin and Prisque. They shook hands all around.

Travis smiled, "If you're wonderin' about the names, Coon Eyes Charlie can see in the dark, just like a coon. Two Pawnees, sneakin' up on him one night, thinkin' he couldn't see 'em, found out that wasn't the case. Bullfrog Kincade, caught a Sioux stone war axe in the throat."

Bullfrog, shook a piece of black hair on his belt, "This here's what's left of that varmint," he croaked out.

"Then, there's Hugo Montgomery. We just call him

Hugo, because there's nothin' special about him," Travis said with a laugh.

Hugo laughed, "The wimmens think I'm special."

Travis laughed, "You just keep tellin' yourself that."

Coon Eyes pointed at the supplies, "Best get yourself somethin' Big Walker, if yuh need it. Rendezvous is clear over in Pierre's Hole this year."

"That is a far piece," Travis replied. He began to work his way into the cluster of men to get a better look of what was in the crates. A young man, dressed in shiny new buckskins, glowered at him, "Best get on back, and wait your turn," he said in a warning tone.

Travis looked at him. The kid was maybe twenty-years-old, a pilgrim with a store-bought set of buckskins. "I ain't takin' your turn, so shut your mouth," Travis snapped back at him.

The kid frowned, but didn't reply.

"You have any Bowies?" Travis asked the owner.

"I do." He lifted up a smaller box and put it on the ground.

Travis lifted the lid to see a dozen sheathed Bowie knives. He took out two, then looked back at Martin and Prisque, "Come and get 'em."

Martin and Prisque went to their saddlebags where their money purses were kept. Martin took out his purse. Prisque pulled up his purse, opened it, but stood staring into it. He held this position for several seconds.

Martin noticed his hesitation, "Do you have money?" he asked Prisque.

Prisque nodded, took out some money, and closed the bag. "Just counting it," Prisque replied. They made their way up to where Travis was standing. The surly kid, who stood several inches taller than Martin shoved him back hard. "Don't push into me, runt."

The immediate gut-punch Martin delivered, drove the wind out of the kid. He wasn't expecting the blow that bent him over double. Martin followed the body punch with a hard fist into the kid's downturned face, splitting his lips open. Martin finished with a fist to the side of the kid's face, knocking him to the ground.

The group of seasoned trappers stepped back as the kid slowly came up off the ground, blood trickling from his lips. He pulled a never before used skinning knife. Leaping at Martin, he awkwardly thrust it at him.

Side-stepping the thrust, Martin locked his elbow around the kid's arm, grabbed the wrist with his other hand, and bore his weight down until he heard the snap of the arm bone. The knife fell, as the kid went to his knees with a scream of pain and shock.

Martin picked up the dropped knife, and pressed the blade solidly against the underside of the kid's chin, whose eyes bugged out, staring into Martin's calm eyes.

"You have very bad manners," Martin said. "You are rude, and offensive. You belong back in the city with your mother feeding you porridge. There is a great difference between being tough, and acting tough. You are not tough, only offensive."

A thin line of blood began to roll down the kid's Adam's apple from the firmly pressed blade. He was trying hard not to cry. "I'm sorry," he whispered.

Martin held the knife in place, "You need to leave, before I become angry."

Travis stepped up beside them. Looking down on the kneeling kid, he said, "You're a youngster, a pilgrim thinkin' that *actin'* tough, is the same as bein' tough – it ain't. Consider yourself lucky, I know a dozen men who would have gutted you for that. Get on that flatboat, and ride it back down to St. Louis. You stay here in this country, actin' like that, and you'll be dead before summer."

Martin pulled back the knife, then threw it into the river. The kid fell forward. Supporting himself with his good arm, he vomited.

The hard, seasoned men, feeling the kid got what he deserved, watched him as they would a sick dog.

He stumbled to his feet, and got on the boat. The owner watched him sit down in a corner and gasp in pain. "I'll drop him off when I head back."

Bullfrog stepped up beside Travis, "Too many of them greenhorns comin' west. Pretty soon the whole country'll be filled up with weak-kneed, lily-livered, mama's boys. Won't be fit for real men 'fore long."

"There's one less now," Hugo said.

They all looked at Martin, giving him an approving eye, "You'll do," Coon Eyes said.

"I believe we were buying knives when I was interrupted," Martin said.

Prisque was holding the two new Bowies. He handed one to Martin. Martin looked at the boat owner, "We do not have pelts, how much in money?"

"Ten dollars each," the owner replied.

Martin and Prisque each handed the man a pair of five dollar gold coins.

"I could use some coffee," Travis said to the owner.

The owner handed him a muslin sack of coffee. Travis paid for it, then walked out of the group of men.

Travis waited with Martin and Prisque while his friends finished trading pelts for the supplies that would hold them until rendezvous.

After they had their supplies, they gathered around Travis, Martin, and Prisque. Martin took Travis' knife off, handed it back to him, and replaced it with his own. He. They all studied the little Metis. Bullfrog looked at Travis, "You can pick 'em good." He walked off to his horse.

"We've got a camp upriver," Hugo Said. "Come on with us. We can ketch up on the past few years."

Travis, Martin, and Prisque headed for their horses. "You handled that nicely," Travis said to Martin.

"He is a spoiled child who never received discipline," Martin replied.

"You could have killed him pretty easily. Why didn't you?"

"He did not need killing, he only needed to be taught manners."

"You're not wrong," Travis said. "He'll remember that lesson for the rest of his life." He stuffed the two knives under the pack tarp, gathered his reins, and mounted the roan. He looked at Martin, "Not all men need killin', just the murderers."

Martin looked back at him, "Foolish young men will never learn manners, or proper behavior, if dead. That young man will remember his lesson. Men like Duncan Black, need killing."

The three trappers headed up river. Travis fell in behind them, Martin and Prisque moved with him. Coming to several acres of willow growing along the river, the trappers entered a dim trail into them. A clearing between the river and willows was thick in green grass. A camp was set in a clear space within the willows themselves.

Prisque asked Travis, "Why are they camped in the trees?"

"It's safer. It's hard for Indians to sneak up on you without making noise, and it's harder for them to see you in there. It also breaks up the fire smoke, so it doesn't give your location away."

Prisque nodded, "That makes sense. What Indians will we encounter here?"

"Not any bad ones," Travis replied. "Maybe, some Omahas, but even when you're in friendly Indian country, it still pays to do everything safe. For one thing, it creates good habits, and for a second thing, you never know when a travelin' war party will cross over. There's a possibility of a hunting party of Pawnees, as we're on the edge of their lands, and they're a tribe, like the Sioux who can go either way."

"Good to remember," Prisque said.

Riding into the clearing, they dismounted, and led the horses to the river to drink. Once satisfied, the horses were led to the edge of the willows where they were unpacked, and unsaddled. Following this procedure, they were picketed in the grass.

Taking their rifles, the three entered the willows where Coon Eyes was bringing a fire up. He looked at them, "Set on down. Just gettin' a coffee fire goin'." He picked up the battered metal pot and shook it, "Got a cup 'r two left in 'er. Only needs more water, and a couple fistfuls of grinds and she'll be up to St. Louis standard." He let out a laugh, as he went to the river with the pot.

"Coon Eyes still make the worst coffee this side of hades?" Travis asked Hugo.

"Worse," Hugo replied. "Last winter, when it was cold as a witch's heart, ol' Beelzebub hisself, come draggin' into our camp. His tail was froze off, he was white with frost-bite, and near to death. He asked if he could warm hisself by the fire, and have a cup of coffee. Feelin' sorry for him, we let him come on in, but kept our knives and tommiehawks ready, 'cause ol' Beelzebub ain't to be trusted. We poured him a cup of Coon Eyes' coffee, thick as tar, and blacker'n a moonless, starless night at the bottom of a well. Whaal, ol' Beelzebub looks at that cup, and says, 'is that Coon Eyes' coffee?' I says it was. Whaal, he up and says, 'guess I ain't that cold', turns and walks away."

Travis laughed, as did Martin and Prisque. "I suspected as much," Travis said. "Even the devil wouldn't drink it, but I guess I got no better sense, so I will."

"You'd best," Bullfrog croaked, "or we'll hear nothin' but crying and moanin' that no one likes his cookin'."

Coon Eyes came back. Digging into his pack he pulled out a sack of coffee grinds. Digging his dirty hand into it, he brought out a fistful and dropped it in the pot. Looking into the pot, he studied it, "Gonna turn out a little thin." He added a second handful to the pot, then set it at the edge of the fire, and sat down with the others.

"Tell me what I missed over the past couple years," Travis said to his friends.

"What was the last rondy you made?" Bullfrog asked him.

"Twenty-nine, on the Popo Agie," Travis replied.

Bullfrog nodded, "Thirty, was up on the Wind River. It was a big one. Bill Sublette came in with Dave Jackson, Jed Smith, and more wagons of goods than you could count. At the end of it, Bill and them, sold out to Gabe, Fitz, Fraeb, Gervais, and Bill's brother Milton. They called their outfit, the Rocky Mountain Fur Company. Come time for the next rondy, in the summer of thirty-one, no one showed up with supplies. Word had it that Fitz went to St. Louis for supplies, but we didn't see him come back."

"What happened to Jed, Bill, and Dave?" Travis asked. "They just leave the mountains?"

"Last we heard; they headed down to Santie Fe. Hear tell, Jed got kilt by the Comanche down there, but we don't know if that's so. We had heard you was gone beaver, too, and it proved not so. For all we know, Jed might come waltzin' into rondy one day."

Travis nodded, "You never know. Word of mouth ain't always reliable."

"Whaal, I'm glad to see we was wrong about you, Travis," Bullfrog broke in. "Good to see yuh back."

"It's good to be back," Travis said.

Hugo looked at Travis over the fire, "You got your vengeance completed?"

Travis looked at him, "To a point, but I won't hesitate to kill any Cheyenne that comes across me."

Hugo nodded, "Can't fault you on that."

Coon Eyes looked at Travis, "Big Walker, it's late in the season, or early, if you look at it that way, for trappin'. Furs not prime now, and it's a ways 'til winter. It ain't trappin' that brought you back to the mountains at this time of year."

Travis shifted his attention to Coon Eyes, "Not lookin' to trap – not yet anyway."

The three trappers looked at him in silence, either he was going to tell them his intentions, or not. They wouldn't pry into his personal business, but hoped he would say something about it."

Travis held his silence for a moment, then asked, "Any of you boys seen Luther Monk?"

Hugo snorted, "*Lucifer* Monk, you mean. That's the lowest snake-in-the-grass in the mountains. I ain't seen him though. Why?"

"I did," Bullfrog said. "He was guidin' a party of nine men. They didn't look like trappers, though. Figured he was up to no good, he always is."

"Where did you see him?" Travis asked.

"Headin' up the Platte, two days back. These boys were in camp, it was my turn to go shoot some meat. That's when I saw 'em."

The three trappers continued to look at Travis, but began to shift their eyes to Martin and Prisque, figuring they played into Travis' return. Martin and Prisque remained silent, if Travis wanted to reveal their intent, it was up to him. They were strangers here, and had to learn the mountain man customs. It was better to remain silent, listening, and learning, then open your mouth and trample on a custom.

Travis looked at Martin sitting to his right, "Okay, if I tell 'em?"

Martin looked back at him, "We will never find them, if we keep it a secret."

Travis nodded his agreement. He looked back at his friends, "Those men Monk was leadin', are a pack of robbin', murderin' scum. They raided Martin's house, molested and murdered his wife, and daughters of sixteen and thirteen years of age. Martin killed one, knifed a couple others, but then they beat him down, thinkin' they'd killed him, then finished their devil's work."

Hugo nodded, "Figgered you was huntin' 'em. No other reason for you to be here in the spring, and wantin' to know about Monk."

"Martin, and Prisque went huntin' for 'em. They were told to find me, that I would help 'em. Martin's wife had shot one of 'em. We found him, and Martin finished him off. We want the rest."

The three trappers nodded in unison. "I'd be doin' the same thing," Hugo said.

"We all would," Bullfrog agreed. He looked at Martin, "Saw the way you handled that brat at the boat. You're a handy man in a fight."

"I know a little about fighting," Martin said.

"I'd say more'n a little," Coon Eyes put in.

They all then turned their attention to Prisque, "You're a mighty quiet man," Hugo said to him. "Are you on the hunt as well?"

"Martin's family was very close to me, as I have no family of my own," Prisque replied. "Their murderers need to be hunted down and killed. I came with Martin to help him."

"Makes you a good friend," Hugo said. "We'll spread the word, that your huntin' them coyotes."

"I would appreciate that," Martin said.

"When it comes to Luther Monk, just follow the men shot in the back, and their outfits stolen," Coon Eyes said.

Travis nodded, "Yeah, he leaves a pretty clear trail."

10

Travis, Martin, and Prisque left the trappers camp in the morning. The three trappers promised to spread the word, so every trapper in the mountains would be on the lookout for Monk's cutthroats. The warning was for the trappers to beware of the murderers and thieves, as much as to let Travis' party know their where abouts.

They followed the Platte west. Massive cottonwood trees, that had overlooked the changing seasons for a hundred years, lined the river bank. Hackberry, cedar, and Russian Olive, filled in the spaces between them. The water source for the tree roots diminished, the further from the river the flat land spread.

Beyond the tree line, the terrain grew predominantly in buffalo grass, and switch grass. Under the sun, the grasses turned brown, however, now, in the spring, the grass was green, with a profusion of brightly colored wild flowers. The land appeared to run flat for miles, then end abruptly, but in reality, the land curved away at the horizon. Should a man keep riding at it, the curve could never be reached, the land remained flat, the curve appearing, once again, in the distance, like a horse who kept moving just enough to keep from being caught.

The river, wide, with exposed sandbars like stepping stones, was steadily drawing down to its shallow summer level. The branches, grasses, and debris caught several feet up in the shoreline trees told the story of how high the Platte ran during its flood stages.

Martin noticed how Travis never stopped turning his head, looking first to the north, then west, and then behind them. He was a man who rode constantly aware of his surroundings. Martin was coming to understand that there were far more dangers here, mainly from the Indians, than the Red River country. He was always aware of his surroundings when he trapped the north country, mostly to watch for bears, angry moose, or the occasional robber. Here, a man's life depended on seeing the danger before it saw him. He found himself emulating Travis' actions.

He glanced over at Prisque, who had said little since leaving the flatboat. He wondered if he regretted his brash, sudden decision to come with him. He actually only knew Prisque from the life of the city. He had met Prisque two years back at the fur auctions. He was starting his own fur buying company, but it wasn't growing as fast as he had hoped it would. They had become friends, having him to supper, and meeting the family. He had fit right in with them.

Prisque told him he had been a Courier on the northern streams and lakes, coming from the country above Lake Ontario. Perhaps his silence reflected his woods nature. Prisque was one to speak when he had something to say, and kept quiet when he did not. Most Frenchmen liked to talk, yet Prisque was never one to over-talk. He was probably fine about being along.

A sound like distant drums disturbed the silence of the prairie. They all looked to the south, where the sound was coming from, and growing louder. Over the curve of the earth came a line of brown objects, running directly at them. Travis narrowed his eyes to get a better look against the glare of the sun, then called out, "Buffalo, and they're comin' at us fast! Get into the trees."

They turned the horses, putting them into a gallop for the safety of the big cottonwoods. The packs jerked, and swayed hazardously on the backs of the pack horses. The thundering grew louder as they reached the trees. Turning in the saddle, Martin was amazed to see the mass of huge brown animals at a full run toward them. He was at once, fascinated, and frightened. The Metis hunted buffalo, the meat was a staple in their diets, and for the making of pemmican, so the animal was no stranger to him, but they did not run in herds of this size. To see hundreds of these beasts, with the thundering of their hooves, and the hurricane of dust they created was spellbinding.

The buffalo had no intention of charging through the trees and into the river. At the treeline, the entire herd made an abrupt right turn, and tore downriver. After several minutes all that was left was a massive cloud of dust that hung in the air, gradually being blown away by the continuous breeze.

Martin and Prisque stared after the animals. "What were those?" Prisque asked, having never seen buffalo.

"Those were buffalo," Travis replied.

"There must have been hundreds of them."

"You should see the big herds," Travis said.

Prisque looked at him, "That wasn't a big herd?"

"Nah, just a few, but if you don't get out of their way, they'll run you right over." Travis turned his attention to study the direction from which the buffalo had come. "Buffalo need something to spook 'em into a run like that," he said. "Sometimes, it's wolves, but most of the time, it's a huntin' party of Indians attackin' a herd."

"Friendly Indians, or not friendly?" Martin asked.

"In this area, we're on huntin' grounds the Pawnee, Arapahoe, Cheyenne, and Sioux lay claim to. Sometimes they fight each other for control. None of them are friendly."

"Will they keep coming this way?" Prisque asked.

"Chances are, they killed all the buffalo they wanted, or they'd still be chasing 'em. Still, I'd feel better if we keep ridin'. Get clear of their huntin' party." He dismounted to reset the pack on the bay. Prisque did the same with the horse he was leading.

With the loads tightened back down, they mounted. Travis pulled one of his rifles, placed a cap on the nipple, and laid it across the front of his saddle. He looked at the others, "Get your rifles out, if we're attacked, that gives us three quick shots. Might be the difference between livin' and dyin'. An Indian don't like the idea that he's the one who could get killed. When a couple fall, the others have a tendency to give up the fight. Blackfeet are the exception, they're too bloodthirsty to give up."

Martin and Prisque copied Travis with their rifles.

"There yuh go," Travis said. He began riding west again, keeping them close to the tree cover in case the Indians appeared.

They rode out the day with no sign of Indians. Two hours before sunset, they made camp in the riverside cottonwoods. Unsaddling and unpacking the loads, they staked the horses on a patch of grass, close to the camp. Travis built a fire, but kept it small, and burning brittle-dry wood, which prevented smoke from giving away their camp. Sitting around the fire, they kept their rifles close at hand, and watched the horses.

While the coffee began to boil, as did a pot of beans, Travis said, "Watch your horses in Indian country. They know when something's goin' on around 'em. If an Indian is sneakin' up, that horse will look directly at him. His ears will flip back and forth, then go straight forward, and his eyes'll bulge, when the varmint is close. If it's a wolf, the horses will start to get agitated, and snuff at the smell. It's a completely different reaction from the sight of an Indian.

Once the horses had finished grazing and were standing half asleep, they pulled the stakes and took them to drink at the river. Then, led them back to the camp, and tied them to the saplings, in close to where they would sleep.

Settling back down, they poured cups of coffee. "I'm curious," Martin began. "Your friends were all wearing buckskin pants and shirts, but you are wearing wool pants and shirt."

"Buckskins are alright in the heat of summer, but for the rest of the year, they're cold and stiff," Travis answered. "Gettin' soaked through from rain, or a river crossin', if not properly tanned, they dry like rawhide. The sun will shrink them to you so hard, you'll suffocate. You have to cut 'em off, and run around buck naked. Wool takes water, and dries without a problem. I've worn buckskins. Sometimes out here, when your clothes wear out, and its months before rendezvous, or a thousand miles from a post, deer or elk hide is it."

"I brought extra clothes," Martin said.

Prisque nodded, "I did, too."

"If things go right, we'll get that pack of coyotes, and you can head back to St. Louis," Travis remarked.

"Nothing for me there now," Martin said. "Just a lot of painful memories."

"Don't let the bad memories push out the good ones," Travis said. "I did that for a long time, and it's a poor return. I'm learnin' to find a balance."

Martin looked at him, and gave a small nod, "I will keep that in mind."

"What are you going to do, if you don't go back?" Prisque asked him.

Martin stared out to the river. It was dark, but the soft sound of the current, along with nightbirds, crickets, and frogs laid a relaxing blanket over the place. "I might just stay out here. I like it." Martin saw this as an opportunity to find out what Prisque's feelings were about the quest. "What will you do?"

"I'm a trapper, and wanderer of the woods – a Courier. I'm an outlaw in Canada because I won't buy their tyrannical license. Out here, I am as free as I choose to be. If you stay, I will, too. We can trap together."

Martin nodded, satisfied in knowing his friend's feelings. "I would like that."

Travis studied Prisque, he was still deciding what to make of him. There were a good many Frenchmen in the mountains, maybe for the same reasons Prisque stated. They were Couriers, who refused to be owned by any man, or company. Unwelcome in a country where men were told to march to a politician's drum, or be arrested. The Rocky Mountains called to such men, and they either sized up, or died in short order. Prisque had yet to show what he was made of, which way he would end up was yet to be seen.

He next considered, Martin. He was a grizzly bear in a small package, but he had met other men like him. He was a Metis, half Indian, but from a tribe that could get along with their neighbors, not kill them. He had heard a little about the race, half French, half Indian, those were the two races, the white Englishmen, who were taking over Canada, couldn't tolerate. He considered the perfect way Martin said his words. His English was spoken a little stiff, and each word pronounced, it was the way men talked who spoke a native language, and learned English.

The little Metis knew how to fight, and he didn't hold back when it came down to it. He showed that with the murdering scum he shot at the fort, and the way he handled that kid at the boat. He carried a secret that he suspected had something to do with his fighting strengths. Martin had suffered a devastating loss, but he knew all about that feeling, as well as the fierce drive to make the guilty pay in blood. He had no concerns about how Martin would stand in a fight.

"Tomorrow," Travis began, "we'll reach the forks of the

Platte. The north fork will curve north, the south fork runs south, then west. The north fork runs through Crow, and then, Blackfoot country, the south fork into that of the Cheyenne and Arapahoe. We'll have to try and figure out which fork Monk takes them. I'm thinkin' the south fork, because Monk would rather face the Cheyenne, then the Blackfeet, but I could be wrong. I'm hoping we come across some other trappers who might have seen them."

"Do most of the trappers know Monk?" Prisque asked.

"Know him, or of him," Travis replied. "He's not welcome anywhere because everyone knows he's a thief, and it's suspected he's responsible for murder, but hasn't been caught at it."

"Is there a reason why they do not deal with him?" Martin asked.

"They would, but he has to be caught at it, if he is, he can be shot, knifed, or beat to death, but not if its only talk, and no one actually sees him commit a crime. As fur buyers, you know that every man handles his pelts in a certain way. It's as tell-tale, recognizable as his face. Monk has been found at rendezvous with pelts that were clearly handled by a trapper who was found dead, and robbed. When challenged about it, he claims to have traded for them from the Indians, therefore, layin' the blame on the Indians for the trapper's murder. They know what he's doin', but you can't kill a man on suspicion, even out here there's some sense of law."

"You said, you caught him stealing a beaver from your trap, and you shot him," Martin said.

Travis nodded, "That's right. I shot him from about two-hundred yards. The ball wasn't fatal, and by the time I got to where he was, he had gotten on his horse and left. My trap, and the beaver were still there, so I let him go. He knows I have the right to kill him, if I choose, because I did catch him stealing from my trap. He wants to stay as far from me as he can."

"He showed up at Fort Osage," Prisque remarked. "He obviously didn't know you were there."

"I think he knew I was there, 'cause he got real mad at the gang for stopping. He had told 'em to keep ridin', but they put in at the fort. He got mighty scared when I called him. He lit out in a hurry."

"Do you think he left the mountains after you shot him?" Prisque asked.

"I don't know when he left. He had to be out to the east, in order to pick up with that gang."

"Won't the trappers see him now?" Prisque asked. "Shoot him for stealing from you?"

"They won't shoot him just 'cause he stole from me. That's another reason I think he will go with the south fork, too many trappers who know him are up on the north fork."

The talk fell off as they listened into the night. "Hear all that night noise?" Travis whispered. "Crickets, frogs, and such. That means, all is well, nothin' has them disturbed. If they suddenly stop, something is movin', and they shut down. When that happens slip back into the shadows and watch for Indians."

"Or, Luther Monk." Martin said.

"That, too," Travis agreed. "It could be a white man. Dangerous, or friendly, either will shut up the night creatures."

"It's a warning," Martin said. "Heed it."

"That's right." Travis chuckled, "I'm preachin' to the choir, ain't I?"

Martin looked at him confused, "What does that mean?"

"It means, I'm tellin' you boys something you already know. You're woodsmen, and trappers."

Martin nodded, "Yes, I do know about the night sounds, but my father gave me a valuable bit of advice when I was just a boy. He said, never listen to the nonsense spewed by a fool, it will make you as foolish as he is, but always listen to a wise man who has the experience to talk. You might be the greatest expert in the world on the thing he is talking about, but if you listen to him, you might learn one new thing you did not know before, and now you know even more about it."

"My father told me the same thing," Prisque agreed. "It's wise advice."

Travis smiled, "Your fathers are smart men. Before this is over, I might learn a thing or two from you boys."

Martin smiled, "Out here, we will be learning from you."

IN THE MORNING they set off upriver. Come noon, they had reached the forks. The narrower south fork of the Platte spilled into the wider north fork. Here, Travis sat on his horse contemplating where to go next. The rasping calls of ravens and crows squabbling came to him. He visually searched the trees to find the birds, finally spotting a great number of them jumping in and out of the cottonwoods a couple hundred yards down the south fork. He understood, when that many of the scavenger birds gathered, and squawked insanely, they were fighting over meat. It might be the remains of a deer, however, with Luther Monk's gang of murderers ahead of them, it could be dead men.

Martin pointed at the squawking birds, "They are fighting over something."

Travis nodded, "Yeah, I've been watchin' 'em. There's something there." He moved his horse down the south fork toward the birds. Martin and Prisque followed.

As they drew nearer, the birds set up a squawk against the human intruders. The birds circled them, not sure whether to land, or fly away, yet refusing to give up the food they had found.

Coming to the spot, Travis dismounted. Pulling his rifle, he said, "Stay here, and stay alert."

Martin and Prisque pulled their rifles, and watched around them while Travis went into the trees.

The moment Travis entered the shelter of the tall cottonwoods he could smell the rotting meat. A dozen vultures hopped away from him, but did not take flight. Dozens of crows and ravens, flew from one tree to another, never ceasing their annoying chatter. He spotted a pair of coyotes slinking back into the woods.

The first thing he saw were two horses tied to trees. They were looking gaunt, heads hanging down as far as the tied ropes would let them. They were clearly dried up, deprived of water for days. He had pinpointed the place the birds had fled from. The abandoned horses told him the smell was that of dead men.

Moving toward a clearing in the trees he could see lumps on the ground. Stepping into the camp he saw two men sprawled out on the ground. The birds had been busy eating all the areas of exposed flesh. It was a grisly scene that attacked the senses.

Walking up to the bodies, he looked them over. There were no arrows, and they were not scalped. That eliminated their being killed by Indians. Their outfit had been rummaged through, clothes, cooking utensils, traps, and other things had been thrown about as if the searcher wanted only certain things. Indians would have taken everything, including the horses. It seemed the only things missing was dry goods. Coffee and flour, were in every trapper's outfit, but there was none here.

The traps told him they were trappers. They had probably been trapping up the Cache la Poudre, and coming back down. This time of year, there should be pelts, but, like the coffee and flour, there were none. It didn't take a scholar to figure out they had been murdered and robbed by white men, and the most likely suspects were the men they hunted.

Walking to the horses, he pulled their halters off, freeing them. What caught his eye were the places that two other horses had stood; they were gone. The weakened animals limped their way to the river, disappearing into the trees and brush. It was his guess, the killers packed the pelts and food out on two of the horses, and left the other two. That meant there had been a lot of pelts. He walked back out of the trees to where Martin and Prisque waited.

"Two dead men in there," Travis said. "It wasn't Indians. Their pelts were stolen, packed out on two horses."

"Sounds like our men," Martin said.

"I'd say that's a safe bet," Travis agreed. "How are you boys at trackin'?"

"Good," Prisque said.

"I can track," Martin replied.

"Good. I'm goin' to search around in here for more sign of who did it. You boys start to look for the trail left by their horses. It should be easy as their horses are likely shod. Most trapper horses are Indian horses, and barefoot. Leave your pack horse with me."

Both Martin and Prisque nodded their understanding. Martin looked at Prisque, "You search down this side of the south fork. I am going to cross over and search the other side, and up the north fork."

Prisque nodded," Okay."

"Keep your rifles handy," Travis said. "We're in Cheyenne country, and there's nothin' friendly about 'em."

The two split up. Prisque rode slowly up the south fork, searching the ground. Martin crossed the stream, and began to scan the ground. Travis went back to the dead men's camp. Dismounting, he tied the three horses to trees.

Standing amidst the scattered supplies, he searched for something that would identify the men. A letter with a name, or a book with the name in it. The faces of the men had been eaten away, so there was no way to see if he knew them. Going through some scattered clothes he found a Bible. Opening it, he found this inscription on the inside cover, *'To dear Warren. Love, Mother.'*

He did know a trapper named Warren. He looked at the back cover and found the man's name, *'Warren Gentry'.* Warren Gentry, he did know him. He partnered with Two Toes Kelly, named for the fact he had stupidly kicked a badger with a moccasined foot, and the enraged creature ripped half his right foot off.

There was one way to tell for sure. Holding his breath against the smell, he pulled the right moccasin off the first dead man. He had all his foot, that meant he was Gentry. Repeating the action to the second body the scarred half of a foot identified Kelly. Now, he knew, and could tell the other trappers what he had found, but unfortunately, there was no proof it was Monk's doing. It was though, and Monk had already signed his death warrant by going in with the cutthroat gang. He walked out of the trees to watch for Martin and Prisque to return.

He could see Prisque searching for the trail. Martin was across the river, beyond the trees where he couldn't see him. Prisque turned his horse back toward Travis. Reaching him, Prisque pointed back behind him, "They kept going up the river. Shod tracks from a big group."

"That would be them." Travis pointed into the trees, "They did that."

"I'm sure they did."

"Go get Martin back here. I'm goin' to start diggin' graves. I knew those men, and I'll not have the varmints and birds eatin' 'em like they were deer guts."

"I'll get Martin back here, and we'll help you dig the graves," Prisque said. He rode to the river, crossed it, and headed for Martin who he could see a quarter mile up the river.

Drawing closer to Martin, Prisque let out a high-pitched whistle sounding like a marmot. Martin turned in the saddle to look at him. Prisque waved for him to come in.

When Martin reached him, Prisque pointed back to the south fork, "I found their trail, they're going up river. Travis learned who the dead men are, he's burying them."

"We need to help him, and then get on that trail," Martin said.

They crossed the river, and rode back into the trees. Dismounting next to Travis' horses, they tied them off. Martin pulled a shovel from the pack, and moved toward Travis who was actively digging a grave. The stench struck them as they continued closer. Neither had ever seen such a ghastly scene as what lay before them, both paused momentarily at the smell, and condition of the half-eaten bodies.

Travis looked back at them, "Ugly, ain't it."

"Horrible," Martin said. "Those murderers have to be stopped before they can kill again."

"Yes, they do," Travis replied, "Problem is, I'm sure they will murder again before we catch up to them."

11

Picking up the trail of the gang, the three continued up the river. The horses had left a pock-marked trail in the dirt and sod, as well as scattered manure. Travis estimated, by the bodies, and tracks, they were two, to, three days behind the gang. Where Monk was leading them was a mystery, but eventually he would figure it out.

The south fork country ran flat and wide, the terrain unchanging from that of the north fork land. Buffalo grass, and blue grama covered the plains, along with the never-ending colors of wild flowers. Hackberry and cottonwood were the dominate trees. Little changed in the terrain between the two forks.

It was a beautiful spring day. The sun was bright, yet a cool breeze reminded the men that winter had not closed up shop all that long before. Winters on the plains were long, with brutal blizzards, and sub-zero temperatures. A man caught out in the middle of a freezing blizzard had little chance for survival. During the winter, trappers tended to group up for safety and companionship.

Fall trapping was the busy time, before the worst of the winter set in, then again in the spring, when the temperatures rose, and fur was at its prime best. The fur was slipping by April, as the animals began to shed their winter coats for the approaching summer. Summers were dry, and hot enough to melt a rifle barrel. Water dried up, and grazing for horses was sparse.

Spring and fall on the plains were seasons to make a man love life, blessing the Creator for such a lovely land. Then, the brutal winters, and scorching summers, made him wonder why he ever came into this God-forsaken land, and why would God create such an inhospitable chunk of real estate. It was a land that showed no mercy, yet bestowed bounty on those strong enough to survive it.

To diminish the joy of spring and fall, and add to the misery of summer, were the hostile Indian tribes. The roving war parties looking for coups, scalps, and to pillage, were everywhere, and anywhere. A man never stopped remembering that. The war parties were generally looking to attack their Indian neighbors because battle was in their blood, and they had to fight someone. Coming across white trappers was a bonus.

Not only could they count coup, the trappers always had guns, powder, horses, and a hundred other treasures.

In the dead of winter, few Indians ventured far from their winter villages. Wars were suspended, as survival was more important than coups and spoils. Their hot blood simmered down along with the temperature. It was hard to get fired up for a fight when you were freezing in a tepee covered in animal hides.

The more friendly tribes, such as the Shoshone, Flatheads, Crow, and Mandan, welcomed the trappers who wintered with them. The trappers had better guns, and weren't selfish about shooting buffalo, elk, and deer and sharing it with the people. They would also fight with the village if an enemy did attack.

It was early afternoon when they found the gangs trail breaking off into the trees. They pulled to a stop, and peered into the shadowed cover. There was nothing to indicate anyone was in there. "Wait here," Travis said, "I'm goin' to look in there to see if they camped." He handed the lead rope to his pack horse to Martin.

Prisque dismounted and began to adjust the pack on the horse, moving some of the shifted items around under the tarp.

Travis rode back out, "They camped here. I want to look it over and see if I can't find something that points the murders to them."

Prisque led his horses into the trees. "I'm taking them to water," he said.

"There's a lot of daylight left, but I'm wonderin' if we shouldn't camp here," Travis said. "Give us more time to search the area."

"Whatever you think is best," Martin replied.

"Let's water the horses first, let them graze a bit, then decide if we should stay here, or not," Travis said.

The horses were led to the river to drink. Bringing them in beside Prisque and his horses. When the horses had drunk their fill, they took them to the grass at the edge of the trees, and staked them out to graze.

Travis looked around, "We're in the heart of Cheyenne country. One of you needs to guard the horses while I search the camp."

"I'll do it," Prisque said. "You go with him, Martin, they might have left something you would recognize."

Martin knew what Prisque meant, but did not want to say it. They might have lost something stolen from the house. He followed Travis into the trees.

Travis and Martin stood still, visually examining the vacated camp. There were two fire spots showing black, charred remnants of wood. The ground around them was flattened, and trampled from walking and sitting men. Charred deer bones were thrown about, tossed away as they ate the meat off.

A splash of whiteish-tan, showed on the ground by a

fire spot. Travis walked to it and pinched up a bit, it was flour with bits of wheat grain in it. "Flour," he said. "They didn't have a pack horse with supplies when they came into the fort, so this is the flour from the pack of Kelly and Warren."

"They did take two of their horses," Martin said. "They packed the pelts and food on them."

"That's what they did alright."

Travis moved on to where the horses had been tied in the trees. Monk was a scoundrel, but he knew how to keep his horses safe from Indians. The ground around the horses was well tramped down by boots. He wondered how skilled this bunch of pirates were when it came to packing a horse. They might have dropped something.

Making a slow walk around the place the horses had been tied, eyes set on the ground, he came on a dried muskrat pelt. Muskrat pelts were small, the fur on the inside, the flesh side out, making them slippery. They could easily fall out of a fur pack if it was too loose. He picked up the pelt, and stood examining it.

Martin walked up to him. Looking at the muskrat pelt he asked, "Did you just find that?"

"Yeah. Layin' right there. Dropped out of the fur pack."

"Let me see it."

Travis handed the pelt to him.

Martin considered how muskrats were skinned by making a cut across the back legs, and the pelt peeled off like a sock. It was then pulled over a bent willow stick frame, fur side in, to be dried in the shape of an arrowhead. "The trapper skinned this muskrat a bit different than the preferred method. See how he made the cut across the front of the rear legs, rather than across the top of the rear legs, as most are cut. This puts an inch of belly fur on the back side. If I see this skinning style on pelts someone has, we will know they are the thieves and killers."

Travis listened to what Martin was saying about how the animal was skinned. "It is a little different, alright."

"He also bent the frame around to form a bottom, then punched two pinholes at the bottom of the skin, and tied a string to them and then to the bottom of the frame. Most trappers simply tie the bottom of the skin to the sides of the frames, and do not make a bottom on the frame. This man has a unique style with muskrats."

"Yes, he has," Travis agreed.

"What I want to know is how do they intend to sell them?" Martin asked. "You said the rendezvous is not until July, and there are no posts to sell to, short of Hudson Bay in the Oregon territory, which is too far for them to go from here."

"Their only choices are to, go back to St. Louis to sell 'em, or wait for the rendezvous," Travis said. "Pickin's are good out here, I can't see them wantin' to leave."

"I am sure they intend to keep stealing furs," Martin went on. "They will have a good many, but they cannot have a dozen horses packing pelts, it would draw suspicion as to where they got them."

"The only alternative they have is to cache 'em," Travis surmised.

"I understand caching. On the Red River, we build caches above ground to keep the animals out. How do they do it out here?"

"You get on some high ground, where there's no chance of water seeping in, and dig a hole big enough to fit a pack of beaver in. Pack the sides good'n hard so it doesn't cave in, put the furs in, then cut a round of sod that fits snug over the hole. Then lay more dirt over it. The hole, if good'n tight will hold the pelts for months. They very well could have furs cached all the way to Pierre's Hole."

Martin nodded, "That has to be what they will do."

"That's my guess."

Martin returned to walking around the camp searching the ground for anything they might have dropped. He began to circle the fire spots, ever widening out the circle, diligently scouring the ground for any item dropped. Coming to a bush with a sharp broken branch protruding out, he spotted two silver coins on the ground. The sharp branch possibly had torn open a man's pocket, spilling the coins without his realizing it. He picked them up, they were quarter-dollar coins bearing the Liberty head on one side, and the eagle on the reverse, 1828 was impressed on the coins.

A bit further under the bush, almost invisible, was a leather pouch, roughly four-inches square. He reached under the bush, and took hold of it. It had something in it that shifted between his fingers. Stepping back from the bush he opened it, then turned it over to empty the contents into his open hand. Out spilled jewelry.

It only took a moment for the stark realization to hit him. He stood stunned, his stomach turning over. In his hand was Odette's wedding ring, her garnet necklace he had given her on the first wedding anniversary they had shared in St. Charles, her mother's locket, and her pearl ring that she wore when they went out for an evening. He sunk to his knees, and began to weep.

Travis, alarmed by Martin's actions, hurried toward him. "Martin, are you alright?"

Martin did not reply. He was leaning over his bent knees, gripping the jewelry in his hand, and weeping.

Travis looked at what Martin clutched in his hand. He could see the pouch in one hand, and a portion of gold chain hanging out from his closed hand. He surmised, by Martin's actions, that he had found something that belonged to his wife, or daughters. He recalled kneeling in the same fashion, weeping, and in such distress he might have easily died. He didn't die, but others did at his hand.

Travis looked the area over. There were horse tracks, and boot tracks, moving past the spot. He narrowed his eyes at the tracks, then looked at where

Martin knelt in his weeping. It was something to keep in mind. He walked out to where Prisque watched the horses. "Something has Martin torn up. You're his friend, go see if you can help him, I'll watch the horses."

Prisque left the horses, going to where he saw Martin crumpled on the ground. Kneeling down beside Martin, Prisque laid his hand over his friend's back. Looking at Martin's clenched hand he saw the gold chain.

After a full minute, Martin sucked in a shaky breath. Wiping his free hand over his eyes, he brushed away the tears.

"What do you have?" Prisque asked softly.

Martin opened his hand, revealing the jewelry. In a shaky voice he whispered, "Odette's jewelry, even her wedding ring. The wretched filth, after violating, and murdering her, took her wedding ring from her dead hand." He sucked in a settling breath, then another, his pain turning to rage, "Oh, I swear," he snarled. "I swear to God in Heaven, I will find this man. I will stick my knife in his belly, and rip him open. I will not stop until I have killed every one of these fiends."

"I'll help you," Prisque said. He scowled at the jewelry in Martin's hand, "We'll kill them all, especially Duncan Black."

Prisque helped Martin to his feet. Martin continued to clutch the jewelry in his hand, with the other he violently threw the leather pouch. They walked out to where Travis stood, rifle held over his left elbow.

Travis' eyes searched Martin's face, seeing the traces on his face where the tears had rolled through the dirt and dust, directly contrasting the fury in his eyes. "Are you alright, Martin?"

Martin shook his head, "No, I am not alright."

"What did you find?" Travis asked.

Martin opened his hand, showing the jewelry. "This is my wife's jewelry, including her wedding ring."

Travis understood that in order to possess the ring, the man had to have removed it from her hand, a hand chilling in death. There was nothing lower that a man would do than that. 'Was it just laying on the ground?"

"It was in a pouch, under a bush."

Travis narrowed his eyes, "Under a bush? Like it was thrown under there?"

"There were two coins there as well. It must have fallen out of his pocket," Martin said.

Travis didn't say it, but thought it odd that the pouch ended up *under* a bush, if it fell out of a pocket. "You know what I would do with the ring? Wear it on a string around your neck, to remind yourself to never give up the chase."

Martin looked at the ring. "Yes, I believe I will do just that. When I find that man, I will show it to him, and then kill him."

Travis nodded, "Sounds like a good idea."

Prisque handed Martin the pouch he had thrown away, "Keep this so you can show it to the man, and ask if he recognizes it. You will see it in his eyes if it's his."

Martin took the pouch and shoved it in his pocket. "I will do that."

Travis looked up at the sun, "There's still some hours of good travel time. We found what we needed here, let's close the gap a little more."

MORNING FOUND them back on the trail of the gang, as it continued along the river. They had covered several additional miles the day before, after leaving the gang's camp. It was hard to tell if they had drawn any closer to their quarry. Robbing the trappers had stopped their progress, but how much time they had gained was the question.

Several hours along, a sense of uneasiness began to creep over Travis. The mountains, and the dangers it presented, created in the mountain man an animal-like sense of apprehension. Knowing something was going to happen before it did. All five senses became acute. Some men could smell danger, be it Indians, or a grizzly bear. Some had vision like a hawk, others, could hear a twig snap a mile away. Travis knew a trapper who could actually press his fingers against an Indian's moccasin print, and tell you how old it was. He had learned not to be skeptical when it came to mountain man senses. No city person would believe it, but the trapper knew better.

Travis sniffed the steady wind like a wolf, there was something on it. They were downwind of the open plains spreading out to their left. He smelled the stirred dust before he saw it. Then, he saw the rising line of dust out on the plains, a half mile out.

Dust, picked up by the wind, was thrown wildly it in all directions, at times forming dust whirlwinds that skipped across the plains picking up debris like a tiny tornado. Dust, rising from a moving buffalo herd, created a cloud, that the wind slowly scattered. Indians rode more, or less, in a single line to disguise their numbers. Their dust rose in a line before the wind caught it. What he saw was dust rising from a long moving line of riders.

Pulling his rifle, he set a cap on the nipple, and rested it over the front of his saddle. Indians, like all men, emitted a scent reflective of their clothes, bathing, or lack of it, and food habits. White men had one scent, Indians, their own. He was smelling Indians now.

Without questioning, Martin and Prisque copied him with their rifles. They looked at Travis, his nose sniffing the wind, he eyes directed out to the open land.

"Get in the trees," Travis said. "Indians coming this way. I'm sure they're Cheyenne. If they see us, plan on doin' some fightin'."

Travis reined his horse into the riverside cottonwoods.

Martin and Prisque followed him. They tied the horses deep in the trees.

"How much powder and ball do you have on you?" Travis asked,

"About ten shots worth," Prisque said.

"Get more out of the pack," Travis instructed. "At least twenty shots. When you fire one rifle, reloaded it fast while keeping the second ready to fire. If they come at us in a rush, and you've fired both rifles, and your pistol, that's what the Bowie's for. Close in fightin'. Don't hesitate to use it."

Lifting the tarp on the pack horse, Prisque pulled out a small keg of powder, and a leather pouch with fifty lead balls in it. He handed them to Martin, then pulled out two boxes of caps. Leaning the backup rifles against a large cottonwood tree, they positioned themselves behind it, and looked out toward the open land.

The dust cloud grew closer until they could see the riders. The line of Indians was long. Travis counted them as they came into view. When the last Indian brought up the rear, Travis whispered, "Forty-two, all men. It's a war party. If they were huntin' there would be squaws, and pack horses."

The Indians continued riding toward the river. Their line would bring them within a fifty yards of the place they stood in the trees. Something stirred in Travis as the Cheyenne drew closer. Their scent filled his nostrils, as his hatred for the tribe steadily rose in him. If not for Martin and Prisque, he would step out and start killing them. He couldn't risk their lives for his vendetta, however, should they be discovered, he would gladly kill as many as he could.

When the Indians were less than a hundred yards out, the war paint on their horses could be seen. The men wore paint, but only a bit that reflected the warrior spirit each possessed. As far as Travis was concerned, their spirits were cowards who would murder an unarmed woman, be she Indian or white, as quickly as an armed man. A dead woman still counted as a coup, and she was scalped. The brave warrior shaking the scalp in the air and letting out a hellish cry, as if he had done some great and death-defying deed, rather than cutting down a woman who carried no weapon. The urge to start shooting was overwhelming. He hoped they were discovered so he could kill them.

One of the Indians in the line turned his head and stared intently into the trees where the men stood. He spoke to the others, causing several to look at the place he indicated. Five broke from the group and began riding toward them.

"Here they come," Travis whispered to Martin and Prisque. "Make sure every shot kills one of the red devils, don't waste a single shot. They're not comin' to parley; they're comin' for our scalps. Get ready to fight."

12

Travis felt the excitement for battle build in intensity as the Indians drew closer. He suspected it was their horses they smelled, or thought they saw. As soon as the horses were seen, the varmints would surge into the trees looking for them.

Travis saw no reason to let them get the jump. "We're goin' to open this ball," he whispered to Martin and Prisque. "I don't want them gettin' the jump on us. I want the surprise in our favor."

Martin, who had faced armed men, and was the survivor, understood the tactic. "Say, when," he whispered back.

The five Cheyenne entered the trees. The lead one spotted the horses, and began to talk excitedly. Travis aimed the Hawken and shot him down. In quick order,

Martin and Prisque each downed an Indian, then quickly reloaded. The remaining two Indians began screaming wildly, running back out of the trees.

The remaining party turned to look at them, having reacted to the gunfire. The two began talking rapidly to the party.

"Nice shootin' boys," Travis said. "He's tellin' them other varmints that trappers are hidden in the trees."

"Will they leave, or come for us?" Prisque asked.

"They'll have to think about it for a bit," Travis replied. "Consult their spirits and gods, hop up and down on one foot, do a bunch of jabberin', throw dust in the air to see how it blows. A lot of superstitious nonsense. Then, a few, who feel their medicine is good today will try it. We'll shoot 'em. Then, the others'll go through a lot of nonsense again. I'd just as soon get it done now."

The lead rider, who appeared to be the war chief for the party, began to walk toward the trees alone. He had left his weapons behind, and walked toward them empty handed.

"What's he doing?" Prisque asked.

"He's goin' to pretend to parley, but what he's actually doin' is sizin' us up. They have no idea how many of us are in here. He's guessin' only three, because only three got killed. He knows the white trapper never misses, but he has to make sure there's just the three of us. He'll figure ten-to-one odds are pretty much in their favor. He'll go back and tell them, and then they'll attack."

Travis stepped out to meet the chief, holding his rifle hip level, pointed at him. The chief stopped and stared at him. Squinting at Travis, he studied him, then with an expression of apprehension, he asked in Cheyenne, "*Háestóhenóéoohe?*"

Travis recognized him, he had been one of those who murdered his boys. The one that got away, running in terror. A gutless, spineless coward. He held a glower of hate on the Indian, "That's right, Háestóhenóéoohe."

The Indian turned to run, shouting out to the party, "*Háestóhenóéoohe! Naxeha! Naxeha!*"

Travis fired. The ball hitting him in the spine, face-planting him into the dirt.

The remaining party began to scream out war cries, and charged recklessly into the trees. Travis had made his way back to his second rifle leaning against a cottonwood. He shot the next one coming in. Martin and Prisque shot two more, then grabbed up the second rifles as the charge left them unable to reload.

They shot down three more, but the war party was stirred into a frenzy to kill Háestóhenóéoohe. Travis let out a resounding mountain man yell as he took a Bowie in each hand and sliced through the first Cheyenne to reach him. "Take that, you murderin' red devil!" He swung the big knives with the ferocity of a grizzly fighting for survival against a pack of wolves. Indians fell to his right and left.

Martin and Prisque were not attacked. They stood

confused for a moment at the fact the Indians were all swarming at Travis, but ignoring them. Their hesitation was brief. Reloading, they shot down two of the Indians attacking Travis. Then, shot down two more, but the Indians still paid them no mind.

Travis was shouting insults in Cheyenne as the Bowies cut through Indians like a sickle through wheat, but the overwhelming number was closing in on him. They were overcoming Travis too quickly for Martin and Prisque to bother reloading. They pulled their Bowies, and waded into the fray.

Indians were lying on the ground, some not moving, others moaning from their wounds. Even with three of them swinging Bowies, the rush of frenzied Indians was becoming too many to stop. Travis' arms were bleeding from knife cuts, but he never ceased shouting insults at the Indians as he ripped them apart with the heavy blades.

The screams of the Indians, and Travis' shouts, made it hard to hear anything else. Suddenly, a rush of men, and gunshots were added to the fray. Martin realized that buckskin clad white men had jumped into the fight. Within minutes, there was not an Indian standing. The bodies lay in various conditions, some shot, others disemboweled, a few nearly decapitated. The incoming rescuers went about finishing off the wounded, and pulling scalps.

The whole episode was a blur to Martin, yet he comprehended that a party of trappers had jumped in to finish the fight. He looked at his hand holding the big knife, both hands were covered in blood. Blood was splashed liberally on his clothes, and he felt the wetness of it on his face. He looked at Prisque, who was equally blood covered.

Travis let out a mountain man war whoop that rolled across the plains, and bounced off the trees. "By the heavens, that was a fight!" he shouted.

"Big Walker!" a man shouted out. "Ain't you got no better sense then to pick a fight with fifty Cheyenne!"

Travis looked at him, "Wiley Thompson, *is that you?*" he called out loudly.

"I have to be, no one else wanted the job!" Wiley replied as he walked up to Travis.

The two men clasped hands roughly. "By Thunder, it's good to see you!" Travis said.

"I thought you were dead," Wiley said. "Everyone was sayin' that Big Walker was killed by the Cheyenne, except those who said it was the Pawnee, Blackfeet, or 'Rapahoe. That killed you"

Travis was beginning to calm down, "Nah, just took some time away from the mountains. Had to do some thinkin'"

"Good to have you back," Wiley said.

Travis looked around to see several trappers scalping the dead Cheyenne. "You leadin' a party?"

"We went down to the Spanish lands. Provost said there was a lot of beaver down that way. There was some down to the south, but the Spanish lands are so dry it takes a week to work up a good spit. No beaver worth mentionin', and them Spanish soldiers told us to get out before they arrested us. We headed back for this country."

"I had heard something like that about the south country," Travis remarked.

Wiley looked at Martin and Prisque, "See you got a couple of new partners. Boys look mighty handy in a fight."

For the first time since the fight ended, Travis looked at Martin and Prisque. They were both covered in Cheyenne blood. He took notice of the sickish look on Martin's face as his eyes surveyed the bloody, scalped bodies. Yet, Prisque, seemed undisturbed by the carnage. There was a story behind that man, as well. Fighting, or killing, was not new to him, but for some reason he pretended it was. "Yeah, they're mighty good men to have on your side," he said back to Wiley.

Wiley went to them and put out his hand, "Wiley Thompson."

Martin shook his hand, so did Prisque, as they introduced themselves.

Wiley laughed, "You boys best watch out ridin' with old Háestóhenóéoohe. He might get yuh killed."

Travis waved his hand over the dead Indians, "Who might get killed?"

Martin took a deep, settling breath. Turning his eyes from the dead, he looked at Travis, "I heard the Indian yell that out, then you shot him. The others starting yelling it, too. It seemed to get them worked up to kill you. What does it mean?"

"Háestóhenóéoohe, means *Kills Many Quickly*," Wiley answered. "They know Big Walker."

Martin studied Travis, it must have something to do with his secret, and his hatred of the Cheyenne. "What does Háestóhenóéoohe, naxeha, mean?"

"Kills Many Quickly – kill him," Travis replied.

Martin, blood covered, simply looked at him.

Travis met his eyes, "That's what the Cheyenne call me. They want me dead before I kill any more of 'em."

"A man's business is his own," Martin said simply. He turned and walked to the river to wash. Prisque followed him.

Wiley looked at Travis, "You didn't tell them?"

"Not yet. I don't like to talk about it."

"Maybe not, but they stood by you. You might wanna consider it."

"Yeah, they earned an explanation."

"Which way you headed?" Wiley asked.

"Up river – so far."

"You're headed in the wrong direction for rendezvous."

"Not goin' there, not right now anyways. Have you seen anything of Luther Monk?"

"Luther *Monk*? Not in some time. Hope he's dead. He

stole from my traps, but I could never catch him at it. Seems I recall, you put a rifle ball in him."

"I did."

"Are you huntin' him?"

"Yeah. He's leadin' a gang of nine murderin' outlaws. They broke into Martin's house in St. Charles, molested and murdered his wife and two daughters. Him and Prisque are after 'em. The gang headed into the mountains. Martin was told to find me, that I would help him."

"Looks like you are." Wiley snorted derisively, "So, they hooked up with Monk, the pile of bear squat."

"He's leadin' 'em. Back down-river we found where they murdered Warren Gentry and Two Toes Kelly. Stole their pelts, pack horses, and food. We're trackin' 'em, and they're headed this way. Don't know why they're goin' this way."

"I do," Wiley said. "Remember, Jory Adams?"

Travis nodded, "Yeah, Rattlesnake Adams, he's as bad an outlaw as Monk."

"Adams partnered up with Monk last summer," Wiley went on. "Warren and Kelly were coming back from Willow Valley, that rendezvous where no one showed up with supplies. Everyone still had their pelts, and thinking they would have to go all the way to St. Louis to sell them. They met up with Bear Bait Jimmy and Nels Smith. They all decided to make the trip in to St. Louis, as they all needed supplies.

"They got down to the North Platte when they came on

Monk and Adams. They had just murdered Frenchie Pelletier, and were packing up his pelts on Frenchie's horses. Well, the boys set after them. Kelly shot Adams and killed him. Monk jumped on his horse and lit out of there at a dead run. They fired some shots after him, but he got away. That was the last anyone heard of Monk, 'til now."

Travis stared at Wiley, "Monk knows Gentry and Kelly worked this area. They didn't come by 'em by mistake. He come huntin' for 'em."

Wiley nodded, "I'd say that's a good bet. Monk knows, if he wants to come back out here, he has to kill them who can prove he murdered Frenchie. He expects to find those four down this way."

"Do Jimmy and Nels still have their cabin up above the Narrows?" Travis asked.

"Last I heard they do."

Travis scowled, "That's why Monk's leadin' that pack of coyotes this way. He'll head up the Poudre next."

"Yeah," Wiley agreed, "to kill Jimmy and Nels. He figures once their dead, he can claim they were lyin' about him, that he never killed anyone."

"That's how I see it," Travis said. "Then, they'll head up the canyon to the Laramie plains, and on to Pierre's Hole, with the stolen pelts."

Wiley nodded, "Likely." He looked around, "You might wanna make tracks out of here before some more Cheyenne come around and find our handy work."

"Yeah, we'd best move on. Tell everyone you meet about Monk, and that gang."

"I'll do that." He extended his hand to Travis, "I'd say, watch yer topknot, but you seem awful anxious to give it to the Cheyenne."

Travis shook Wiley's hand, "I ain't *givin'* 'em *nothin'*! If they take it, they'll pay a mighty high price for it."

Wiley laughed, "See you at Rendezvous – maybe."

"Might be there, depends on what Monk does." Travis watched as Wiley gathered the party. They mounted and continued down-river. He turned and walked through the trees to the river.

Martin and Prisque were kneeling at the edge of the river washing their arms and faces. He stripped off his shirt, knelt down beside them, and began to wash as well. He winced as he washed the blood off the cuts on his arms, the cuts continued to ooze blood, but the cold water was slowing the bleeding. "I want to thank you men for jumpin' in there and helpin' me. I was beginnin' to think I wasn't comin' out of this one."

"You looked like you were in trouble," Martin said.

Prisque sat back on the bank, "I'm still shaking."

Travis looked at him, recalling Prisque's unaffected countenance. "That's the rush of blood. Makes you shaky when the fight's over."

Prisque nodded, "Probably. I have to admit, I was scared."

"Only a fool wouldn't be, but you sure never showed it," Travis replied as he ran water over the cuts.

Prisque arched his forehead, took a deep breath, and released it, "Well, I was. That was a new experience for me."

Travis nodded, but didn't respond. It might have been the first time Prisque was swarmed by Indians, but he knew how to fight, and death didn't seem to shake him.

Martin, stood up and looked at Travis, "They wanted to kill you in the worse way. They ignored us, but swarmed all over you. Why is that?"

"We need to get shuck of this place before more Cheyenne show up," Travis said. "Let's get a long way from here, and then we need to talk about the past." He looked at Martin, then to Prisque, "All of us."

Martin nodded, "If we expect to survive the Cheyenne, we need to know why they want to attack us at every opportunity."

"I would like to know why you left your people," Travis said. "The Metis are not wanderers. If I'm to help you hunt these men down, I need to know if there's a reason that bunch went after you."

"I will tell you what I know. We have bandages in the pack. Let me bind up those cuts."

"They'll be fine, we need to get goin'."

"We do not need you leaving a blood trail, or bleeding

to death," Martin argued. "Ten more minutes is not going to matter."

They walked to the horses. Martin pulled a box from under the tarp, and removed lengths of cloth bandage. He wrapped seven bad cuts on Travis' arms.

Travis looked at the bandages, "That does feel better, thanks." He looked out toward the open plains, "Let's get outta here."

13

T he shadows were growing long across the river
when they stopped for the night. They had put
several hours, and at least twenty miles between
them and the place of the battle. Finding a sheltered camp
in the riverside trees, they tended to the horses. It was dark
when they took the horses to the river for a last drink, then
tied them to the trees by the camp.

Sitting around a small, smokeless fire they poured cups
of coffee.

"Okay," Martin began, "why do they call you . . . that
word I cannot pronounce."

"Háestóhenóéoohe," Travis answered. "It means, Kills
Many Quickly."

"How did you come by that?" Martin asked. "Why are
they so determined to kill you?"

Travis took a settling breath, this was hard for him, but maybe he needed to give it some air. Perhaps, saying it out loud would ease the pain and pressure inside of him. "I'm originally from Tennessee," he began. "We were hill-folks, made my livin' at odd jobs, but mostly trappin', and huntin' for meat markets. I had a wife, two daughters, and twin sons, Alan and George. The boys were the oldest, they trapped and hunted with me."

He paused, hesitant to say it, but, he had to say it, the words had been bottled up far too long. "The girls were twelve and ten when small pox swept through the hills. My wife and girls caught it . . . and died. It missed the boys and me, maybe because we were out in the woods so much. I had to get them out of there before they caught it to. I buried my beloved wife, and girls, then headed my boys west, to get as far from civilization and its diseases as we could.

"We had brought our guns, traps, and other things on a packhorse. In St. Louis we outfitted for the Rocky Mountains, and went on west. That was in twenty-two. There were a few trappers out here then, but they really didn't start to come in until twenty-four with Ashley's brigade. That opened the gates, and more trappers came west. We had pretty much stayed north, between the North Platte and the Yellowstone. There were a lot of streams to trap, Knife River, Tongue, Big Horn, Green, all filled with beaver and otter.

"The first two years we brought the pelts back to St. Louis to sell. It was a long trip, and it scared me because of the sicknesses the boys might pick up, but we got out okay. In twenty-five we sold them at Ashley's rendezvous on Henry's Fork. That was the start of the rendezvous tradin'.

"We had trapped amongst the friendly Indians, Kickapoos, Mandans, Snakes, Crows. We learned to stay on the south side of the Yellowstone, or run into the Blackfeet on the north side. Stayin' on the west side of the Missouri kept us out of Sioux country. We got to know the country like no one else, 'cause we had been out here first. I eventually came to accept the loss of my wife and daughters, thankful to have my boys safe with me. We had also come to love our mountain life.

"As the trappers became more plentiful, the boys and me, got to be well known. Everyone liked the boys. They laughed a lot, made friends, and were good companions. There were a few times we had fights with Sioux, and Blackfeet, who came over into Crow country. The Crows hate both tribes, and liked it when me and the boys fought with them."

Travis refilled his cup, wiped a hand over his face, and settled back. He was silent for several seconds then began again. "By eighteen-thirty, beaver was growin' thin up in that country, too many trappers. We were told that the Laramie plains, Medicine Bow mountains, and south fork of the Platte had been lightly trapped. Since we liked to explore new country, we headed down this way. We knew that it was Cheyenne and Arapahoe country, and they didn't care for white men, but they weren't as bad as the Blackfeet. That was natural for the life of a trapper, we knew to be careful, but if you were scared of Indians all the time, you might as well head back for the disease-infested cities.

"We crossed the north fork of the Platte where the south fork comes in, the place we passed a while back. We kept ridin' south across the Laramie plains, toward the Medicine Bow mountains we could see in front of us. We made our camp on the upper fork of the Laramie River. We were in Cheyenne country, but we hadn't seen any of 'em. The river had a lot of beaver on it, but it was too early to trap, but we could still scout traplines for the fall.

The next mornin', the boys wanted to scout for fur sign. We needed meat, so I went out to hunt while they scouted. I got to wanderin' up a stream lookin' for beaver, gone longer than I had expected to be. I shot a deer on the way back. Gettin' to the camp, the boys were still gone, but I figured, like me, they had got caught up followin' beaver sign. Time passed, and I started to get worried about them, so I set off on the trail they had left."

Here, Travis stopped talking. He stared into the fire, his bearded chin visibly beginning to quiver. He was locked into this position for a pair of minutes, clearly fighting back the pain and tears. Martin and Prisque remained quiet, allowing Travis his silence. They had a good idea what he had found.

"There was no reason for it," he whispered in a shaking voice. "They weren't hurtin' anyone. There was no reason." Dragging in a ragged breath, Travis let it out shakily. "It was the birds I saw first. Crows, ravens, they were gatherin'. The fear choked me. I knew what I was goin' to find. I saw him layin' there, before I got close. It was Alan, he had twenty arrows in him, and he was scalped. His gun, horse, and everything was gone. I got off the horse, and picked him up . . ." Travis broke down weeping.

Martin knew the pain his new friend was going through. He felt it every day.

Wiping his arm across his nose, and then his eyes, he said in a small voice, "I broke all their accursed arrows off, and laid him over my saddle. I saw nothing of George, or his horse. He would not have left his brother, so I knew the devils had taken him. I brought Alan back to camp, laid him down and covered him with a blanket. I went back to pick up the trail of the murderin' devils.

"I found 'em. I could see their camp, alongside the river trees. There was a bunch of the wretched fiends. I pulled both rifles, and rode into their midst. They had George tied to a tree, shootin' arrows into him, and laughin'. From the saddle I shot two of the devils. I came off the horse, my eyes filled with the blood of fury. Pullin' my knives, I waded into 'em like a mad man. I was cuttin' 'em down as fast as I could. They thought I was an evil spirit, and started screamin' in terror. I killed 'em while they ran around like the cowards they were. A few escaped. I let 'em go, knowin' I would find them, and cut their guts out.

"I took George back to camp. Laid him beside his brother, then set out to kill the ones who had escaped, and then to kill every accursed Cheyenne coward in the country. I went back to their camp, and counted fourteen that I had killed. I tracked the others, caught them on their horses, and shot two of 'em off. The others galloped away as fast as they could. I went back and buried my boys.

"After that, I spent the rest of the summer huntin' Cheyenne. They came to call me, Háestóhenóéoohe – Kills Many Quickly, because of how fast I killed fourteen of the accursed devils. Over the summer, I killed at least twenty more. They were terrified of me; thought I was an evil spirit. That Cheyenne that came to scout us was one of the ones who escaped. He recognized me, panicked when he saw me, calling for his pack of cowardly curs to kill me. They probably thought they were free of the evil spirit of Háestóhenóéoohe. Kills Many Quickly, was back, and killing 'em."

The last part of the telling had raised the fury in Travis. He sat still, fighting down the insanity that would renew his drive against the entire Cheyenne nation. Taking a breath, he said, "Come winter I headed back east. I made it as far as Fort Osage, and settled in there. I didn't want to be around people. I wanted to be left alone with my pain and misery. I had killed the accursed red devils. It did not bring my sons back to me, but they paid, oh, they paid." He looked up at Martin, "When you told me your story, I knew I had to help you. Those cutthroats must pay in blood, just as my son's murderers paid in blood."

"Now, I understand," Martin said. "You killed those who murdered your sons. Do you intend to keep hunting down the Cheyenne?"

Travis shook his head, "No. I won't go after 'em, but if they come for me, I'll gladly kill every one of the accursed varmints."

Martin nodded, "Fair enough. Now, I understand what to expect, and why."

They fell to silence for several minutes as Travis stared out into the dark woods, regaining his composure. Turning his head, he stared at Martin across the fire. He didn't say it, but it was in his expression. It was Martin's turn to explain."

"At the forks of the Red and Assiniboine rivers," Martin began, "the Cree, Nakota, and Ojibwe lived since God made the rivers, the French trappers and voyageurs, came to live with them in the sixteen-hundreds. They inter-wed, and so the Metis race was born. The forks was the main rendezvous site for trade, long before Hudson Bay, or the Northwest Fur Company arrived. In eighteen-and-nine, the Northwest Company built Fort Gibraltar. Many of us traded with the company, and they were welcome.

"Four years later, the Earl of Selkirk, a Scotsman, still in Scotland, sent a colony of indentured Scot farmers to the Red River, and planted their colony right at the fork of the rivers. They were each promised one-hundred acres of *our* land at the end of their indentureship.

"No one consulted the Metis, or Indians, who lived there. They just came in, and took over. The colony blocked an important provisioning route for the Northwest Company, so they objected to it, but the Earl of Selkirk did not care. The Northwest Company's voyageurs depended on the pemmican made by the Metis, for their main food. It was a staple of their diet. Pemmican was regularly taken by canoe to the voyageurs in the woods.

"As the Red River Colony, as it was named, grew, they appointed a governor, Miles Macdonell, who was given control over all of us, not only their colony. Naturally, we refused to cooperate with being taken over by these usurpers. We learned that Macdonell and the Earl were owners in the Hudson Bay Company, which explained how they gained control so quickly. Needless to say, there was bad blood between the Scots and Metis. They often shot at us, and we would shoot back.

"The final insult was when Macdonell issued, the *Pemmican Proclamation*, an act that prohibited the Metis and Northwest Company from taking pemmican out of the colony, which now included us. It was nothing more than a corrupt ploy to control the Metis, and refuse the staple food the voyageurs working for the Northwest Company needed, thus destroying Hudson Bays competition.

"A Metis leader, and employee of the Northwest Company, was Cuthbert Grant. Under Grant's leadership, and the backing of the Northwest Company, we escalated our demands for the colonists to get out, as we had no interest in being governed by these squatters. Instead of giving in to our demands, Hudson Bay seized Fort Gibraltar, and commanded that we ship no pemmican to the voyageurs, or conduct trade past the colony. They even set up gunboat blockades to keep us from using the river.

"Grant, not one to give in to the demands of Hudson Bay, and their corrupt leaders, formed an overland party to run the blockade by horseback, and deliver the pemmican to our men at Fort William. I was with him, there were at least sixty Metis and Indians in the party. We were at a place called Seven Oaks, when the Hudson Bay Governor, a man named, Semple, stopped us with thirty, or so, armed men.

"Representatives of both sides began to argue, then one of Sempler's men fired on us. Then, one from our side fired back. Sempler's men raised their rifles to soot us, but because we were woodsmen skilled in fighting, we all dove to the ground as they fired at our group. They thought, because we were on the ground, they had killed us. They took off their hats, waved them in the air, cheering our deaths. However, we were not dead. We came to our feet and shot down several of them. We then went to hand-to-hand fighting. In short order, twenty-eight of Sempler's men, and Sempler himself, were dead. The few left ran away.

"I had shot, and killed one, then reloaded and fired again; I am sure it was my rifle ball that struck Sempler. We went on to make our pemmican delivery. When we returned to our homes, we were informed that the British government had called for our arrests for murder. I knew there was no justice for the Metis against the British rule, as they despised us entirely. I was the one who killed the Hudson Bay governor. I was sure to be hanged.

"I gathered up Odette, Sharice, who was a small child, and took us south, out of the reach of the British authorities. For three years we lived in trapping camps, collecting pelts, saving money until we reached St. Louis. There I intended to build a fur buying business, but found the business was controlled by a few wealthy men. We continued on to St. Charles, where I bought our house, and begun my business."

Travis nodded, "I can see why you got out of there fast. I don't blame you a bit. So, how does Duncan Black's gang play into this?"

"I am not sure. When Duncan, and the man now dead, came in to sell the pelts, I thought he was familiar, somehow, I knew him. It wasn't until the ferry operator said he heard the men call him Duncan, that I suddenly put it together. It had been years since I last saw him. He was one of the free Scots controlling the indentured farmers, and a Bay thug, but there is no reason why he would come after me. I never had any problems with him myself."

"Do you think, it was just because he knew you had money, being a fur dealer? It was simply a case of you being his target?" Travis asked.

"I think it was. It was just coincidental that he picked me to rob. He was sizing me up that day he came in to sell the pelts. It was when Odette came downstairs, and they saw her, that he got the idea to do the rest."

"They might have been planning to rob you on the way to St. Louis with all your pelts for the auction," Prisque suggested. "They came in that day to see what you had."

"That is possible," Martin said. "It would have been difficult to get away with that, as I was on the busy road the whole time. It seems they would be smart enough not to try it on a traveled road."

"Here's a question for you to think on," Travis said. "If it was the furs they wanted, and they knew you were at the auction, why did they wait until you had returned home to attack? The furs were gone by then."

Martin furrowed his brow, as he considered the question.

"I had not considered that," Prisque said, "but, here's a possible answer. It would be easier to steal the fur money, than the furs. They waited for you to come home with the money, then attacked. I'm sure, after seeing Odette, they intended to do the rest at the same time."

Martin looked at him, "They did ransack my office, and took the small amount of money I had in the strongbox. They *were* looking for money. They thought to kill me, and take the money. That is more plausible than robbing me of a wagon-load of furs."

"They didn't know, that I had your money," Prisque said. "So, they did not get the money they came for, however, they could not leave any witnesses after thinking they had killed you."

"There is one other consideration," Travis said.

Martin looked at him, "What is that?"

"It has nothin' to do with furs or money. Duncan did know you, and was sent to kill you. When the men broke through your door, and you started to fight, did you see Duncan in the group?"

"No. It was fast and crazy, I was not able to see them all, but I recall some faces, and his red beard would have been easily seen. He was not in the first attackers."

"He came in after the initial attack," Travis said. "He let his underlings take the first shot, then came in when it was safe for him. He saw you bloody on the floor, and assumed you were dead. Mission accomplished. They then went on with the rest. You were dead, and since they couldn't leave witnesses, they killed the women, but took their pleasure in doin' it."

"If killing me was his purpose, why did he not kill me when he was selling the pelts to me?" Martin asked.

"The time wasn't right. First, he had to scout it out, and see if it was really you. Then, he knew to come back."

"How would he know where to find me in the first place, and secondly, when I would be back from the auction," Martin asked.

Travis looked him in the eyes, "Someone told him. You, and your family, were setup."

Martin gaped at him, his eyes showing shock at the idea, "By who, though? I have no idea who would do that, and for what reason?"

Travis held the look, "I can think of a few reasons, but I'm pretty sure we'll learn the truth in time."

They fell to silence as each became lost in his thoughts. After a quarter of an hour, Travis looked at Prisque, "What's your story?"

Prisque gave him a surprised look, it was clearly a question he had not anticipated. "I have no story to match those of you, and Martin. I was a courier, an outlaw in the eyes of the British who controlled the fur trade. I went south to trap, as a free man. Then, began a fur buying business. That's my story. Nothing special about it."

Travis held a look on him, "You handled yourself pretty good in that fight with the Cheyenne. You know how to shoot, and use a knife."

Prisque shrugged, "There is nothing to that. I have been

shooting since I was a boy, but I don't see why you think I handled a knife that well. My knife skill has been limited to skinning, and dressing game, I have never used a knife for fighting."

Travis knew there was more to his history, but if he wasn't willing to reveal it, that was his business. He nodded, "Okay."

14

Sleep came hard to Martin that night, as his mind ran over-and-again what Travis had said about his being set-up by some unknown person. He lay, staring up at the stars, his right hand clutching Odette's wedding ring hanging from a leather string around his neck. It was possible Duncan Black was sent by Hudson Bay to kill him, but it had been seven years since the Seven Oaks fight, why did he come now?

Maybe, it took Black that long to find him, but if his quest was to kill him, why murder and rob along the way? How would he even know where to find him? A house, among many, in St. Charles? Yes, he had a fur business, but he was not that widely known. What person, who knew him, was close enough to this cutthroat gang, to send Duncan to him, and for what reason? He could not think of anyone. He had come to respect Travis' keen awareness, and insight, there had to be something Travis saw, that was eluding him.

It was pointless to keep thinking about it. He could guess and speculate forever, and he would still be at the same place, not knowing why Duncan Black came for him. When he finally caught up to Black, he would demand to know, then he would kill him.

His thinking drifted to the Indian fight. He had never experienced such insanity in human beings. The Indians were in an absolute frenzy trying to kill Travis. They were so intent on him, they completely ignored him and Prisque, as they continued to shoot them. He suspected it all came back to the superstitious nature of the Indians. The Cree had their gods, rituals, and superstitions as well, but he never saw them go into a killing frenzy like those Cheyenne did.

He could still feel his arms swinging the big knife, meeting the resistance of flesh and bone, then plowing right through it. The sensation gave him a slight shiver. The Bowie knife was indeed a formidable weapon.

This world was far removed from all that he had known, yet he was coming to like it. He had yet to see the Rocky Mountains, they were supposed to be magnificent. There must be something about them to make men give up all the lures society offered, in exchange for the traps, knives, and guns of the mountain man. To forever live on the alert, or perish. To fight Indians, and brutal weather, to be lucky to survive one more day, let alone a year. He knew the lure of the trapline, and love of the woods, what was out here must be a thousand times stronger. In the days to come, he would have answers to a lot of things. Tomorrow was another day. One day closer to finding the men he hunted. He closed his eyes.

It was mid-day when they came to the place the Cache la Poudre River emptied into the south fork of the Platte. It was a sparkling blue, clear stream that wound down from the pine and spruce shrouded hills to the west. They could see the course of the stream across the flat prairie.

"This is the Cache la Poudre," Travis said. "It got its name from a party of French trappers who had to cache their powder here. The trappers just call it the 'Pooder'."

Travis rode up the Poudre a short way, searching the ground. Yeah, just like I thought, they're headed up this way, he said to himself. He waved for Martin and Prisque to follow him.

Martin and Prisque left the south fork behind, as they followed Travis up the Poudre. Through the day they stayed on the stream. Martin was enamored with its clear water, riffling over a rocky bottom, and how cold and pure it was to drink. Reaching the base of the hills late in the day, they stopped for the night. The river wound out of sight, into the rugged hills.

The next day they rode into the canyon of the Poudre River. At the lower end, the rocky hills rose above the river, sparse in vegetation except for pines, their roots clinging stubbornly to the earth that was more rock than dirt. A worn Indian trail followed the river.

The further they got into the canyon, the higher the steep slopes grew, until they stood hundreds of feet above them. Brush, and stunted pines, clung to the near vertical slopes where slick shale rock ran in fans down to the trail. Here the river rushed down with whitewater intensity. Martin and Prisque leaned their heads back to look up at the high walls that closed them in, and laid the trail in shadow.

"The Narrows are a couple of miles up," Travis said. "There's no passage through, it's where the canyon walls squeeze the river into a rifle barrel, and blast it out like a shot. That's why the water here is running fast, it's still got speed from the Narrows."

"How do we get through, then?" Martin asked.

"There's a trail that goes up, and over, the Narrows. It's a steep climb, but it's the only way into the valley. It's a beautiful valley, and worth the climb."

"Will Monk know that trail?" Prisque asked.

"He does," Travis replied. "He'll take them over, but whether those men are up to the ride, is the question."

"Do the Indians come up here?" Prisque asked.

"They generally don't," Travis answered. "They have everything they need down below; they don't see any reason to kill themselves going over the Narrows. Once in the valley, we should be able to relax a little from the Indians."

"Have you been up here much?" Martin asked.

"We ran our trapline through the valley a few years back. That's where I caught Monk stealing from my trap."

"Monk must spend a lot of time up here, to know the trails," Prisque remarked.

"It's a good place to hide out, and avoid other trappers. It's easy to get into the valley from the north end, off the Laramie plains. That's how he gets in and out, but he knows the Narrows trail."

"You said, two trappers live up here, that Monk might be after," Martin said.

"Yeah, Bear Bait Jimmy, and Nels Smith. Hopefully, they're okay."

The rode on until the surge of water through the sheer rock walls of the Narrows could be heard. "Is that the Narrows I hear?" Martin asked.

"Yeah." Travis pointed to a bighorn sheep trail, across the river, ascending the steep dirt and rock hillside. "That's the trail."

Prisque frowned, "Our horses will be able to go up that?"

"It's slow going, but they can do it for a ways, then we'll

have to get off and lead 'em. I ordinarily would have gone into the valley from the north end, but Monk led them this way. So, this is the way we had to go."

Prisque continued to stare up the hillside, "We have no choice."

"I want to see the water squeezed through the Narrows," Martin said.

Travis shrugged, "A few more minutes won't make a difference." He led them on upriver.

The streambed steadily narrowed, the canyon walls closing in until the sun could no longer shine on the river, or diminishing trail. The rush of the river, turned completely into white-capped rapids, shot down toward the prairie below. Ahead, they could see the vertically straight walls of rock ending any further passage. Here the river had to ram its way through an opening only a few feet wide. The water, pure white with pented-up power, shot into the air, dropping with a crash to the widening stream below.

The roar of the water was so loud they could not speak to each other. They stared at the exploding water for several minutes, then Martin gestured for them to ride back down to where the trail started up the hillside.

Getting back to where they could hear, Travis said, "That's the Narrows. You can see there's no gettin' past it."

"That is an amazing sight," Martin said. He looked up at the trail, "We should start."

Travis led them across the fast flowing, but shallow river, climbing out of the water, the trail immediately began to climb. He pointed at the horseshoe, chewed dirt of the trail, "They came this way, alright."

"If they can do it, we can, too," Martin said.

The horses heaved themselves forward, their necks stretched forward for balance. The trail proceeded at an angle across the hillside, not straight up, yet ever upward. Coming to a level stretch of fifty feet, Travis stopped to let the horses catch their breath. "We need to get down and lead 'em from here. It's too hard on 'em packin' us and climbin'." He looked back at Prisque, "Tie the pack horse to the saddle, he'll follow."

Prisque worked his way around the horses on the narrow trail. He looked nervously down, one misstep, and he would roll all the way back to the river. He clung to the horses as he tied the pack horse to his saddle.

Taking the roan's reins, Travis started walking up the trail. The bay pack horse balked until the tied lead rope had his neck stretched to its full length, then he began to follow the roan. Martin came up next, Prisque behind him.

They were sweating, and exhausted, when they reached the ridgetop. Far below, the river was a white and blue thread. The water blasting through the gap between the rock walls, looked to be no more than a squirt from a bottle. Here they sat, and caught their breath.

The cool spring breeze blew through the surrounding

spruce trees. Frozen patches of snow lay under the shadowed evergreen trees, reminding them that winter had only
recently retreated from this high country. The breeze
cooled them quickly. Once the horses had rested, they
mounted and rode on.

The trail led over the top of the ridge. The tracks of the
gang were plain to see in the dirt, and duff shed off the
pines. Their tracks were the only ones on the trail. Travis
stopped on the ridge where the trees opened to allow a
view of the Cache la Poudre valley below. The river wound
through a wide expanse of green meadows. Groves of
aspen dotted the landscape, and formed borders between
the meadows and timbered hills.

Martin stared out over the scene, "Magnificent," he said
in a low voice. "I have never seen country such as this.
What are those huge trees with the orange bark?"

"It's one of my favorite places," Travis said. "Those are
ponderosa pines, they're all over these hills. Wait until you
stand next to one, makes you feel mighty puny."

"I have never seen trees like those," Martin said with a
hint of awe in his voice.

"We start down from here. The trail down is a lot easier
than the one goin' up." He moved the roan on.

The trail descended a gentle hillside through the white
barked aspen, their bright green, heart-shaped leaves shim-
mering, and shuttering in the breeze. They crossed the

slow flowing river, and out onto the meadow. Travis led them alongside the stream.

"Jimmy and Nels, have their cabin up here about half a mile," Travis said. "I know those boys can take care of themselves, but so could Gentry and Kelly. I'm sure they thought it was a party of trappers, until they saw Monk, and then it was too late. Jimmy and Nels would think the same thing."

The cabin was across the river where it made a wide bend away from the hills. The cabin was built into the tree cover, pines and aspen to the rear, and sides, the front was open to give a good field of view. A trail of smoke drifted out of the stovepipe. "Someone's in there," Travis remarked. He moved the roan across the river. Martin and Prisque followed.

Travis stopped fifty yards out from the cabin, "Hello, the cabin," he called out.

A minute passed before Bear Bait Jimmy opened the door, in his hands was a rifle. "Who's callin', and what do yuh want?"

"It's Travis Walker, Jimmy."

Jimmy stepped out away from the cabin for a better look. He leaned his head forward trying to make out the man on the horse, then cried out, "Whaal, I'll be a greenhorn pup, if it ain't! Come on in. Come on in!"

Travis heeled the roan forward. He dismounted and shook hands with Jimmy.

"Why, we all thought you was dead, Big Walker!" Jimmy cried out with excitement. "Everyone at the last rendezvous said it was so. You disappeared, and we figured the Injuns had finally took yer skelp."

"Nope, just took some time away from the mountains," Travis replied.

Jimmy smiled, revealing several broken teeth, "The return of Travis Walker. I can hear the tales now. Boy's'll be spinnin' 'em from here to the day Gabriel sounds his trumpet."

Travis smiled, "I don't think they'll remember me for that long."

"What brings you this way? Just to visit?" Jimmy asked.

"There's a purpose. Have you had any trouble the past few days?" Travis asked.

"Why, as a matter o' fact we did have a bit of shootin', two days back."

"Luther Monk?" Travis asked.

Jimmy stared at him, his mouth slightly open, "Yeah, it was. How did yuh know?"

"Where's Nels."

Jimmy jerked his head toward the cabin, "Inside, he took a pistol ball to the leg. He's okay, but laid up for a spell. What's goin' on Travis?"

"If you've got coffee, I'll tell you. It's a long story."

"Whaal, where's my manners," Jimmy shouted out.

"Come on in." He looked at Martin and Prisque, "Who's your new partners?"

Travis pointed at each, "That's Martin, and Prisque."

"Frenchmen? I know some good un's. Come on in." Jimmy turned and headed for the cabin.

Martin and Prisque dismounted, and followed Travis leading their horses.

Jimmy walked through the cabin door, "Nels, you ain't gonna believe what I just found."

Nels was sitting in a chair, "Prob'ly not, if it's one of your wild yarns."

Travis stepped through the door, "I've been called a lot of things, but never a yarn," he said to Nels with a laugh.

Nels gaped at Travis for a second, then he let out a whoop, and tried to jump to feet, "Oww," he shouted, and dropped back down in the chair. "A thousand curses on Luther Monk," he snarled as he pressed down on the leg. He looked up at Travis, "You ain't a ghost are yuh?" he chuckled.

"Nope, it's me, flesh and blood."

"We all heard you was gone beaver. Ol', Kills Many Quickly, was just a scalp on a Cheyenne's coup stick."

Travis snorted, "You think some stinkin' Cheyenne could take this scalp?" he lifted his hat to reveal the mop of brown hair.

"It'd be a handsome trophy for some Cheyenne buck,"

Nels chuckled. "The scalp of Kills Many Quickly'd make him some big muckidee-muck in the tribe."

"Travis knew Monk was here," Jimmy said to Nels.

Nels looked at Travis, "How'd yuh know that?"

"I'll tell you in a minute, first, what happened here with him?" Travis asked.

"Whaal, Luther Monk come ridin' up, bold as brass, with a pack of curs," Jimmy began. "We heard 'em ride up, and figured it was a party of trappers stoppin' to say hello. Whaal, Nels opens the door, and Monk shoots Nels right then and there. He was the last person we expected to see in these mountains, after what he'd done. I grabbed my rifle, and shot back at him, but he moved, and I shot too fast, and missed him. They scattered like fool hens, and I got Nels back into the cabin."

Travis nodded, "We ran into Wiley Thompson down on the South Platte. He told us about you, Gentry, and Kelly comin' on Monk and Adams fresh from murderin' Frenchie Pelletier."

"That's right, we did," Nels agreed. "Kelly shot Adams dead. Monk took off like his hind end was on fire and his head was ketchin'. We fired at Monk, but he was gallopin' so fast he out-run the rifle balls. Haven't seen him since, 'til now."

"That's because he went to hidin' back in the states," Travis said. "He's back out here now, like you found out the hard way. We found Gentry and Kelly murdered in their camp, and their pelts stolen."

"That's terrible!" Jimmy burst out. "Cheyenne?"

Travis shook his head, "Monk, and that pack of coyotes, did it."

"Are you sure it was Monk?" Jimmy asked.

"Yeah, we've been trailin' him, and that gang."

"He did have a bunch of reprobates with him," Nels said. "Worthless scum."

"Did they kill Gentry and Kelly just for the pelts?" Jimmy asked.

"Wiley figured, and I agree, it's because they could prove Monk murdered Frenchie. If he killed the four of you, he could deny the murder, by sayin' you were lyin' about him. No one would believe him of course, but there was no proof if you were all dead. He came up this way because he knew Gentry and Kelly worked the South Platte, and you had the base camp up here."

"You mean, he come huntin' them, and us, to shut us up?" Nels asked.

"Yeah, and to steal pelts," Travis answered. "He knows everyone will be holding their winter's catch for the rendezvous."

Nels snorted with disdain, "That sounds like that horse turd, Monk."

"Okay, what happened after he shot Nels?" Travis asked.

"I didn't want to go out, and get shot," Jimmy picked up the story. "So, I barred the door, and closed the Injun attack shutters, and looked through the cut-outs. A few rifle balls hit the cabin, so they was out there. I spotted one of them varmints sneakin' up, and I shot him. It's hard to get a decent shot through that little hole, and I only winged him, but he skee-daddled out of the way.

"Nels got his britches off, and wrapped a bandage around the wound. The ball had went plum through, without hittin' the bone, so that was a bit of good luck. I figgered they was here to steal our pelts; I hadn't considered that other business you spoke of. Anyway. I figgered, they'd wait 'til dark, then rush us, or smoke us out. Whaal, there weren't no point in settin' and waitin' for that, so I slipped out the back door, into the trees, and started huntin' 'em.

"I spotted one, and shot him. He went to hollerin', and cryin' to beat the band. That brought the pack runnin' to him. I fired at 'em, hit someone, I know 'cause I heard a yelp, and they lit a shuck outta here. Jumped on their horses, and skee-daddled. I saw Monk in the pack, I fired at him, hit his horse, but it didn't go down. That was the last we seen of 'em."

Travis nodded, "But, you hit three of 'em."

"Yup, don't know how bad though. They was able to ride outta here."

"That's 'cause you're the worst shot in the Rocky Mountains," Nel's put in.

"Not, so," Jimmy came back, "It's jist my eyes don't see so good no more."

"Was one of the pack a man with a big red beard and red hair?" Travis asked.

Nels nodded, "There was. When I opened the door, he was in the front row, on a horse next to Monk."

"I'll tell yuh one thing," Jimmy broke in, "they's the biggest bunch of lily-livered cowards I've ever seen. They was all big and tough until I started shootin', and then they was runnin' like rabbits with a dozen wildcats on their tails."

"Monk's a coward, always has been," Travis said. "I aim to shoot him dead, the next chance I get."

"I hit his horse, that oughta slow 'em down," Jimmy said.

"Knowin' how they are, I'm sure he took one of the wounded men's horses, and put him on foot," Travis said. "If the others were too injured to keep up, they'll dump the lot of 'em. They did it before. Wounded men slow 'em down, and dumpin' one, two, or three off, makes the cut richer for each still up and ridin'."

"That was two days ago," Jimmy said. "If, like you say, they dumped 'em off, and they're walkin' wounded, you should catch up to 'em quick enough,"

Nels looked at Travis, "Okay, Travis, now tell us why your huntin' this pack o' dogs."

Travis looked at Martin who had remained silent, taking in the account. "You start with your part, and then I'll finish with what I know."

15

At first light, Travis, Martin, and Prisque were riding north through the valley. An hour from the cabin they spotted the circling buzzards in the distance. The black birds were circling lower with each revolution. Drawing closer, they could see the usual collection of crows and ravens darting down to the ground, then flaring back into the air.

A large brown hump lay on the ground. A half-dozen coyotes padded around the hump afraid to approach the pair of wolves eating on the thing. "Must be the horse Jimmy shot," Travis said.

Riding up to the dead horse, the buzzards on the ground, jumped into the air. The wolves growled at the intruders, but Travis' shouts caused them to run off a short distance. They stopped a hundred feet away, and watched the men.

Travis studied the dead horse from his place in the saddle. The saddle was still on it, but the saddlebags, and rifle with scabbard had been removed. "I doubt, Monk is walkin'. He took one of the wounded men's horses. We should find that one before long. Even one of that gang, would have sense enough to follow the river."

As they moved past the horse, a coyote rushed in to grab a bite. The wolves immediately ran in attacking the coyote, the animal yipped loudly, and ran off. Martin was watching the interaction of the canines. "We do not have coyotes on the Red River, but I can see why you compare the cutthroats, and Monk, to coyotes. They are slinking, cowardly, animals."

Travis nodded, "Just like they are. Coyotes are only brave when they think they can get away with something before being killed by the strong animals."

They rode at the water's edge, Travis studying the grassy and sandy bank. Stopping the roan, he stared at a place in the sand. He dismounted, and looked closer at two depressions, side-by-side, in the sand. "Two men laid here, drinking water. There's blood spots in the grass. So, there's two of 'em on foot, and they're bleedin'."

"It shouldn't be hard to get on them, if they're moving slow," Prisque remarked. "We should be able to finish off another two members of the gang."

"We should," Travis agreed. "They can't move as fast as men on horseback, even with a two-day head start. The worse off they become, the slower they'll get, and the more they'll stop."

Travis looked up the river, where it wound through the valley. There were plenty of places for them to hide in the trees, however, if they were hurting, they would want to return to civilization, so they would keep moving as best they could. That is, until they dropped from hunger, and blood loss.

He wondered if they were woodsmen, or city men. Woodsmen would have some idea how to take care of themselves. They might even have a possibles bag with flint and steel for a fire. Snare wire to catch food, a knife, and possibly a pistol. If they were city men, they would have nothing, depending on Monk to take care of them. The man they threw off at the fort had a possibles bag, but was too sick to use anything in it. Mounting up, they continued along the river.

As they rode out the day, storm clouds began to gather. Black clouds were pushing the blue, and fair-weather white clouds ahead of it, bringing the chill of an approaching storm. "We're in for a big rain," Travis said. "We'd best get in under the spruce, these storms blow up wicked, and cold." He untied his coat from behind the saddle and put it on. Martin and Prisque did as well.

To give credence to Travis' words, the first flashes of

lightning darted out of the black clouds. With the flashes came the low rumble of distant thunder. Travis led them across a grassy meadow, toward the low hanging boughs of the tightly growing spruce trees on the hillside.

It was the wind scattered smoke coming out of a hill-side grove of aspen that caught Travis' eye as they crossed the meadow. He pointed at it, "That might be our men there."

Travis shifted his route toward the aspen. The storm was rolling closer to them, the lightning snapping brightly against the black sky, the thunder growing louder. He debated whether to take cover first, and then check out the smoke, or go directly to it. He kept going toward the aspen. He wanted Gentry and Kelly's killers.

A hundred yards from the aspen, they could see two men, one lying down with no blanket, the other sitting by a smoky, green wood fire, nervously searching the sky. "No one would be up here without horses, or an outfit," he said. "They have no blankets, and don't have sense enough to get under the spruce instead of the aspen. That's them."

"And, they are burning green wood," Martin added. "They started a fire, but do not have sense enough to burn dry wood."

A bolt of lightning slammed into the far end of the meadow, filling the air with the smell of its fire, followed by a rolling boom of earth-shaking thunder. The first splats of rain struck their faces. They were within sight of the men now.

Prisque looked up into the storm, "We don't all have to go get them. Give me your pack horse and I'll get the supplies under cover."

Travis looked at him for a moment, "Thought you wanted to be in on the kill?"

"I came to help Martin find these men," Prisque replied. "Martin has the right to kill them. We found them, now I'm thinking about our supplies."

Travis handed Prisque the rope to his pack horse. "Get under the spruce. We'll be along."

Prisque took the lead rope, and moved his horse up the hill, into the protection of the spruce. Travis watched him go.

Martin looked at Travis, "What is the matter?"

Travis shook his head, "Nothin'. Let's go talk to these men."

Their approach was covered by the thunder, and heavy rain drops striking the ground and rattling the aspen leaves. They dismounted, tying their horses to aspen saplings at the edge of the grove. Martin took Odette's pistol out of the saddlebag, and slid it between the buttons of his coat, to keep the powder dry.

They stepped into the sparse camp from the rear of the sitting man, then stepped around to the front of him. The man jumped startled, then let out a cry of pain, settling back down on the ground. He stared up at them.

"Mighty sparse camp," Travis said loudly over the storm. "No coats, no blankets, no food, no horses."

The man who was lying down, rolled over, and sat up, looking at them. The rain poured through the thin branches of the aspen, causing the fire to sputter, and die.

"You're not mountain men, or woodsmen, or you'd have an outfit, and not be stupid enough to make a fire under aspen in the rain," Travis went on. "You look like the curs who tried to attack two men in a cabin back down the river. Seems a couple of them got shot, and you boys look kinda shot up. What do yuh think about that?"

The two men sat still, not answering. They looked at Martin, who was studying them, trying to place the faces of the men who broke into the house. The man by the fire was one of first wave that attacked him, that had to make the man with him, another of the gang.

"You vermin attacked my home, raped my wife and daughters, and murdered them," Martin said in a calm, yet deadly voice.

"The man sitting, began to shiver from the cold, and fear. "I have no idea what you are talking about."

"Liar. We have been following you for days. You are with Duncan Black."

The sitting man made a quick glance at the other man. A gesture that revealed their knowing Duncan Black.

"Yes, I know Duncan Black," Martin said. "Did Hudson Bay send you, or was it the Red River colony?"

Both men stared at Martin, the rain running off their faces, but it could not cover the realization in their eyes that Martin Ouimette knew all of that.

"You were shot by the men you attacked at the cabin," Martin went on. "You were wounded. Luther Monk's horse was shot. We found it dead. He took your horses and threw you off because you were slowing them down. Tell me I am wrong."

"Okay," the sitting man said. "Duncan, and that other man, wanted us to help them get the women, I refused. I was willing to steal the money, but not attack the women."

"What other man?" Martin demanded.

"I just know his name is Dupre, that's all. He was a friend of Black's. They did business together."

"Shut up!" the other man shouted. "He's got nothing on us. Keep your mouth shut."

Martin looked at the sitting man, "I do not know anyone named Dupre. What business did he have with Black?"

"I don't know a lot about it. He had known Duncan from times before."

"Why did you come after me?" Martin demanded.

"The money. Dupre knew you, wanted you dead. Said there was money from the furs. He wanted the woman, too."

"You are lying. You were in the house. You were one of the first to attack me. I cut your arms repeatedly."

"I'm not lying! There was a man named Dupre who wanted it done."

"Push up your sleeves!" Martin demanded.

The man hesitated.

"You don't have to do that!" the second man shouted at the first man. He can't prove anything."

Travis lurched forward, ripping the man's right sleeve from his shirt. Across his arms were three recent, deep knife cuts, scarring over. Without a word, Martin pulled the pistol from inside his coat, cocked the hammer, and shot the man in the head. He fell back onto the smoldering fire.

The other man sat gaping at the dead man, shocked to his core. Dropping the pistol, Martin pulled the Bowie. Slamming his boot into the man's chest, he drove him hard into the ground. With his foot on the man's chest, pinning him to the ground, Martin leaned over him, and shouted, "Did my children cry out? Did they scream in terror?"

The man gaped up at Martin, frozen in fear. His eyes wild with the realization of his coming death.

"Did you cut their throats as they cried in fear? "Curse you! *Curse you to hell!*" Martin screamed as he swept the big knife down with all the fury pent up in him, nearly severing the man's head from his body. Blood spurted and flowed as the man's body jerked, stiffened, then sunk down in death.

Martin stood over the dead man, the rain pouring down on him, his fury seething in and out with each hissing breath. "Curse you," he whispered.

Travis stood watching him. The little Metis was a grizzly bear. He was harboring as much hate and vengeance as he had for the murders of his sons. Nothing will drive a man to kill faster than the justice he would dispense on the men who senselessly murdered his children.

Martin stepped back away from the body. The rain had soaked his hat, drooping the brim over his ears. Water poured down his face and hair, his coat and pants soaked through, but he took no notice of it. He had slain two more of the creatures who murdered his wife and beloved children.

As they stood under the aspen, the black storm clouds were moving eastward, behind them, blue sky filled the void they left. The last spatters of rain fell, then stopped, yet the water dripping off the aspen leaves continued to rain down on them.

Martin stood, his head down, the bloody knife in his hand. "My children," he sobbed. "My dear babies."

Travis put his hand on Martin's back, "I cried a bucketful of tears for my boys, it's okay."

Martin nodded, sniffed, and wiped the back of his wet hand across his nose. "How frightened they must have been," he whispered.

"There's three who knew fear before you killed them. There's seven more, we're thinnin' 'em down."

Martin still looked at the ground, "He said there was another man involved, a man named Dupre."

"That's what he said. "He wanted you dead, and wanted your wife. He knew you, and her, at least in passin', or in business. Maybe he's the one from the colony that was sent for you, and he's using Duncan's gang to do it."

Martin lifted his head, and looked at Travis, "I have no idea who it could be. I do not know any man named Dupre, at the Red River, St. Charles, or St. Louis."

"He knew you, and your family"

Martin scowled in thought, "I can think of no one named Dupre, yet, I am sure if he came from the colony, he would know me, and Odette."

"Hopefully, we will find out who he is, and he can join the dead ones," Travis said.

"We would have to go back to St. Louis to find him, and that could be impossible."

Travis shrugged, "If he worked with Duncan Black in the past, and present, what's to say he won't come out here to join him. You can get the whole collection of 'em."

"That is possible." Martin looked at the knife, then wiped over the wet grass, and across his leg, and slipped it back in the sheath. He picked up the pistol, it was well soaked. "I will have to give this a thorough cleaning before I can load it again."

Travis knew Martin's attention wasn't on the gun, it was on the mystery of this Dupre, but the gun was something he could put into words. "Yeah, you'll want it bone dry, before putting powder down the barrel."

They walked to the horses. Travis swept the standing water off the saddle seat with his hand, then mounted. Martin put the pistol back in the saddlebag, then mounted. They rode up into the trees where Prisque had taken the pack horses.

They found Prisque under the shelter of several huge spruce trees, their heavy, spreading boughs eight feet from the ground, formed a perfect rainproof roof. He had the horses unpacked. Prisque looked at them, "Were they the ones?" he asked.

Martin dismounted, "They were. One had the cuts I gave him at the house. Both had been shot by Jimmy."

Prisque nodded his acknowledgement. "Are they dead?"

"Yes. The one did say an interesting thing, though," Martin said.

"What was that?"

"He said there was another man with them, a man named Dupre. He was with them at the house. He said Dupre is the one who wanted me dead, and to go after Odette."

Prisque frowned, "Dupre? Do you know a Dupre? I cannot think of anyone by that name."

"I cannot think of anyone named Dupre, either. How

would he know enough about my family to deliberately target them? He said, Dupre did business with Black, and had known him from days before."

"Could this Dupre be someone from the colony, or Hudson Bay?" Prisque asked. "An old enemy, you might have forgotten about?"

"Dupre *could* be associated with the Red River colony, or Hudson Bay, and was in St. Louis. Being a regular at the fur actions would let many men, who I do not know, see me. If Dupre bought their stolen furs, he might have been one to sell at the auctions. I did not know everyone there. He might have been waiting for Black to arrive, so he could come after us."

"But, if he was from that colony, and wanted you for the shootings, why go after the women?" Travis asked. "Seems, he would just kill you."

"There is always the chance he lied to you," Prisque said. "There was no other man, no such person as Dupre. He just said that to save himself."

Martin nodded, "That is entirely possible. He *is* a liar. He lied about being at the house, he could lie about a man named Dupre, as well."

"I would say that is more plausible," Prisque remarked. "Aside from the colony, or Bay men, you don't know anyone by that name, or who in St. Louis had a vendetta against you."

Martin furrowed his brow for a long moment as he

considered the possibilities. Finally, he said, "There was no other man, he lied about it." He then walked off to gather fire wood.

Travis stood quietly, listening to the exchange, his eyes going from one to the other. It was his thinking that there *was* another man named, Dupre. Someone had to know Martin, and his family, well enough to set up the whole affair. It was also his thinking that Martin was not convinced Dupre was a lie.

Travis looked at Prisque, "What if there was someone else in that pack, who knew Martin, but Dupre isn't his real name. Someone had to have given information to Black regardin' Martin's family and business."

Prisque raised his hands, palms out, "I don't know. It's all so horrible. All I can think of, it goes back to the Red River colony, and Martin being involved in that gun battle. As far as his life in St. Charles, everyone liked him. I never heard anyone say a cross word against him. Why would someone want to kill him?"

"Fur tradin' is a cutthroat business. We especially see it out here between the fur companies. He might have been in someone's way, or they wanted his business. It might be this Dupre, or whatever his name is. By using a false name, Martin would never know who it was, even if he was standin' right in front of him."

"That is possible, of course," Prisque replied, "but, why

attack his family, if they wanted to kill him for his business?"

"It wouldn't be the first time a man lusted after another man's wife, but couldn't have her. They went in to kill Martin, but why not take the wife at the same time? Working with that pack of coyotes, who haven't a shred of moral fiber, they would take the girls as well. Then, all the witnesses would have to die."

Prisque stared at Travis for a long moment, a perplexed expression on his face. "The worst part of that is, it's entirely possible."

"No," Travis said, "the worst part is, Martin isn't dead like they thought, and now, he's out for blood. *All* the blood."

16

The afternoon following the confrontation in the aspen, they topped out on the last ridge before breaking out onto the Laramie plains. Looking across the plains, the land spread out before them. Sage, juniper, and buffalo grass, green from the recent rains, covered the ground. Through the heart of it flowed the Laramie River. To the west, the Medicine Bow mountains, still showing snow on the peaks, rose to fill the view. To the east, a herd of buffalo could be seen grazing on rising and falling land that looked like a rumpled floor rug. To the north the plains rolled on.

"This is Crow country," Travis told them. "If we see any Indians, they'll likely be Crow, 'cause they don't let Cheyenne or Sioux poach on their huntin' grounds, but both are known to challenge the Crow by trespassing. If caught, the Crow will be quick to attack."

"You said the Crow were friendly," Prisque said.

"For the most part, they get along with the trappers. They'll steal your horses if they can, 'cause, to their way of thinkin', if a man is so careless as let his horses be stolen, then he doesn't deserve to have them."

"Where do you think Monk will lead them now?" Martin asked.

"I have to think on that," Travis replied. "He's got himself a big problem. He failed to kill Jimmy and Nels, and they're witnesses to his murdering Frenchie Pelletier. He's goin' to have to go careful, try to avoid them, or eventually kill them before rendezvous."

"Why before rendezvous?" Prisque asked.

"At rendezvous, Jimmy and Nels will spread the word to everyone. Monk will have to leave the mountains again, or someone will shoot him. Most trappers liked Frenchie."

"He is stealing pelts along the way," Martin said. "He has to sell them at the rendezvous, so he has to go there. He will be seen then, yes?"

"Yes, he has to go there, but not necessarily seen," Travis replied. "This rendezvous is supposed to be a big one. The big ones in the past were spread out over a mile of country, sometimes more. Several fur traders come in, and set up all over it, but way-far apart so their competition can't see what they're gettin', or givin' in trade. A trapper can go from one to the other 'til he finds one that gives him what he wants. Monk could go to one on the outskirts of the thing, sell, and get out.

"I'm thinkin', he'll wait on the upper Snake River, north of Pierre's Hole. Since this one is in the British held Oregon country, Hudson Bay will be settin' up for trade. They aren't much liked by the other traders, and a lot of the trappers won't trade with Hudson. "'Cause of that, Hudson will set up on the northern, or western edge, close to the Snake River, away from the other traders. Monk will watch for Hudson Bay to set up, go right to them, sell, and head out."

"As much as I hate Hudson Bay," Martin said. "It would be smart to go directly to them, and watch for Monk, and the gang."

"That's a good startin' point," Travis agreed.

"How long will it take to get to Pierre's Hole from here?" Prisque asked.

"Two, three weeks, of easy ridin', or ten days of hard," Travis answered. "No point in goin' hard at it. The gatherin' won't be until July, and it's only May now. We still need to try and find that gang. Monk knows he has plenty of time to kill trappers, and steal the pelts, before then."

"We want to stop that, if we can," Martin remarked.

Travis scowled at the thought of Monk killing more of his friends. "We have to."

They dropped down off the ridge to the plains below. Riding through the sage they kept their eyes roving over the plains. It might be Crow country, but the trespassing Cheyenne, or Sioux, wouldn't hesitate to attack them.

The ridge was an hour behind them when Travis spotted a party of Indians riding toward them from the east. He squinted his eyes to see them better, by their clothes and horses, he could tell they were Crow. "Crow party to the east," he said.

Martin and Prisque looked to the east and saw them. "What can we expect?" Prisque asked.

"They won't attack, that's the main thing," Travis replied.

The Crows saw them, and turned in their direction.

Travis stopped his horse. "They're comin' to check us out. Just sit nice and calm, they're not a threat."

As the Crow drew closer, Travis said in a low voice, "It's a scoutin' party. They're patrolling the border to make sure the Cheyenne haven't crossed over."

Travis recognized the party's chief. "I know the chief, he's a friend, and he speaks good English."

The chief smiled when he saw Travis. "Kills Many Quickly!" he shouted out. "We had heard you were dead. The great killer of the Cheyenne had been killed, and scalped, by a lowly digger Indian. It was said, he caught you eating his bugs and worms, and he killed you with his worm digging stick."

Travis laughed, "It's good to see my old friend, Arrows Cannot Harm Him, hasn't lost his sense of humor."

Arrows Cannot Harm Him, gave Travis a serious look, yet his eyes danced with humor, "I was not making a joke. I believed it. You are so weak, from eating bugs and worms, that a digger could kill you with a stick."

Travis shook his head, "And, you accuse the Sioux of being untruthful."

Arrows Cannot Harm Him, burst out laughing. He put his hand out to Travis, and they shook hands. "We did hear you had been killed. I'm glad to see, it isn't true."

"I just left the mountains for a while, to think."

Arrows Cannot Harm Him, nodded, "Yes. If my sons had been killed by my enemies, I would also kill them all, then go to the mountains to be alone. Have you killed anymore Cheyenne since you came back?"

"A few," Travis answered.

Arrows Cannot Harm Him, nodded, "Good. Do you have their scalps to show?"

Travis sneered, "I would not want one near me. The constant stench of Cheyenne would sicken me."

"Let them rot with their scalps, then," Arrows Cannot Harm Him, remarked.

"Are you scouting for trespassers?" Travis asked.

"Yes. The Cheyenne, and Sioux, have been trespassing. We caught a hunting party of Cheyenne killing our buffalo. They no longer have a need to eat."

Travis nodded, "Killed 'em all, did yuh?"

"All of them."

"Good."

"Are you going to the rendezvous at Pierre's Hole?" Arrows Cannot Harm Him, asked.

"We intend to."

Arrows Cannot Harm Him looked Martin and Prisque over, then at the pack horses. "You have no pelts. You didn't trap?"

Travis shook his head, "We are hunting a party of white men." He pointed at Martin, "They killed his wife and daughters, we have come to kill them. There were ten, we have killed three of 'em, but the rest are staying ahead of us. There should be eight in the party now."

"What do they look like?" Arrows Cannot Harm Him, asked.

"Do you know who Luther Monk is?"

"Yes. He is a thief, and a coward."

"Yes, he is. He's leading that party, killing trappers and stealing their pelts. The chief of the party has a big red beard, and red hair."

"I haven't seen him," Arrows Cannot Harm Him, answered. He looked back at his party, speaking in the Crow tongue, he asked if any had seen these men.

Two of the party nodded, then spoke in Crow.

Looking back at Travis, Arrows Cannot Harm Him, said, "Those two were making a scout apart from the party, and they saw eight men, and one had a bright red beard that shined in the sun. They were going north."

Travis nodded, "Working their way toward Pierre's Hole." He looked at Arrows Cannot Harm Him, "It was good to see you, old friend, but we need to get on the trail of these men."

"Yes. You must kill them. It's good to have you back to help us kill the Cheyenne," Arrows Cannot Harm Him, said with a grin. "Kills Many Quickly, will have them wiped out by summer."

"Maybe not by summer," Travis said with a laugh. "We're goin' up out of their range, but maybe we can kill some Blackfeet for you."

"That would be good, as well. I will see you when you come back to kill more Cheyenne. We will join you."

Travis nodded, "We'll do that." He heeled his horse, and started riding north."

The Crow party swung back to the east.

"The good part is, we have a direction, now," Travis said to the others. "The bad part is, I expect to find someone dead before we reach the Sweetwater."

"That is not encouraging," Martin remarked.

"No, it's not. They're killing friends of mine. I knew Warren Gentry when he first came to the mountains. He rode with the boys and me for a while. After a couple years, he partnered up with Brian Kelly, that was before he kicked the badger, and earned his new name, Two Toes Kelly. I don't want to find any more of my friends dead."

Veering to the northwest, Travis led them across the

sage covered plains. Throughout the day, they did not come across another trapper, or Indian. At the end of the day, they made camp beside several large, gnarled juniper trees.

"Why is it, we have not seen another person all day?" Martin asked. "Should there be some trappers about?"

"Right now, most of the trappers are holdin' up in their camps," Travis explained. "They're restin' from a long, hard winter, and just finishin' the spring trappin'. They'll start out for the rendezvous next month."

Martin frowned, "That certainly makes it easy for the gang to kill them in their camps, and steal the furs."

"Unfortunately, it does," Travis replied. "Trappers are usually alert for dangers, but come this time of year, they tend to stay out of hostile Indian country, and relax. Feelin' safe from Indians, they let their guard down. A group of white men ride up, they think it's a party of trappers, and invite 'em in. Too late, they learn it's a pack of murderin' robbers, but then they're dead."

"Monk knows that, too," Martin said.

"Yes, he does. I hope to get him within rifle range, and put an end to him."

THE NEXT DAY they came on to a slow-flowing river. "What river is this?" Prisque asked.

"We're back to the north fork of the Platte," Travis answered.

"I thought the north fork flowed east and west," Prisque remarked.

"No, what it does is make a big horseshoe," Travis began. "It dumps into the Missouri, from the west. We followed it west, then broke off onto the south fork. If we had stayed on the north fork, we would have gone north. It makes a horseshoe, then goes back south into the mountains. Actually, it's the other way around, it starts in the mountains, and ends up in the Missouri, but the big horseshoe is still the same, and we would have ended up in this same spot by goin' upstream."

"We just made a big circle," Prisque said.

"That's right. Give the horses a rest and a drink," Travis said. "I'm goin' to look up and down the river, to see if they crossed here."

Martin and Prisque dismounted, while Travis rode on downstream. "They sure are an elusive bunch, aren't they?" Prisque remarked.

"Yes. There is a lot of country for them to lose themselves. I had no idea the country out here was so vast. If not for Travis, I would have no idea where to go."

"We would never find them," Prisque said. "Then, they would return to St. Louis, and go back to their criminal business, while we spent the rest of our lives wandering out here looking for them."

Martin looked at him, "Do you wish you had stayed back in St. Louis?"

"No. These men have to be found and killed. If I had remained back there, every day I would be wondering about you. No, I'm glad I came to help you, even though I'm not killing them, I can still help you find them."

"I appreciate your companionship. You are a good friend."

"I was getting bored in the city, anyway," Prisque remarked. "I'm happy to be back out in the woods. I haven't trapped in a few years, and I would like to be back at it."

"What about your fur business?"

"It's finished for the season. Most of the pelts to be had now will be sold at the rendezvous. The spring season is finished, and all my pelts have been sold. I have nothing left in my warehouse."

"You do not want to go back to your fur business?"

"Not so much. I thought it would be a good way to make money without all the hard work of trapping, however, I came to find it dull. Colleting the pelts myself was hard work, but it was more interesting than counting them in my warehouse."

Martin nodded, "It can get dull. I must be truthful; I do like being out of the city."

"I might go back one day, but not in the foreseeable future," Prisque added.

They let the horses drink, and waited for Travis to return.

A half hour passed before they saw him riding toward them from upriver.

"They crossed down there about a quarter mile," Travis called out to them. "Some unshod Indian horses, likely Crow, have been along the river. A wide spread pattern of shod tracks crossed the river. Figurin' the different trails they left, I count 'em as eight, so that's our boys."

Martin and Prisque mounted, and followed Travis. Where the gang had crossed the slow-moving river, they crossed as well, the water coming to the bellies of the horses. Reaching the opposite bank, they continued riding; however, Travis was riding across the tracks, showing interest in them.

Travis rode back to them, "Something's goin' on with this bunch. They're ridin' spread out from one another, rather than in a line, or closely grouped like they had been."

"What does that mean?" Martin asked.

"Hang on, I'm goin' to check something out."

Martin and Prisque watched as Travis rode back and forth across the horse tracks, then round them. He would stop and study a spot, then move on to study a different spot. Seeming to be satisfied with what he saw, he rode back to them.

"What did you figure out?" Prisque asked him.

"They're startin' to fight amongst themselves. They

might not like the way Black and Monk are abandonin' their friends, or fightin' over the cuts of fur."

"What makes you think they are fighting?" Martin asked.

"First off, until today, the tracks have been in a close group. Now, the tracks are spread way out. An indication they don't want to be next to each other. That usually happens when partners start gettin' annoyed with each other, they separate. I've seen that a time or two when trappin' partners are on the outs. They avoid each other by ridin' apart. That's what these are doin'. Second off, they're startin' to pair off. I see where two sets of tracks are next to each other, apart from the others."

"They're still heading in the same direction, though," Prisque said.

Travis nodded, "They are. They have to if they want their share of the pelt sales at Pierre's Hole. Still, that doesn't mean they won't change direction to rob a trapper. We have to stay on the trail, no matter where it leads."

"Then, we keep following them," Martin said.

"We do," Travis replied. He moved his horse on.

THE NEXT DAY, they came to the Sweet Water River where it emptied into the Platte. The scattered horse tracks crossed the Sweetwater, then began to merge together again. The land in all directions was flat, with sparse grass. Barren buttes rose up out of the flat land like giant brown dogs curled up asleep. Trees were scarce; however, the merging tracks were headed toward a stand of cottonwoods between the river and a butte.

"This can't be good," Travis muttered. He kept riding toward the trees. As expected, crows, magpies, and ravens were gathered in the trees.

Martin was coming to understand how the birds and animals behaved in this wilderness. "Those are scavenger birds," he said to Travis. "Like where we found Gentry and Kelly."

"Yup," Travis answered, tight lipped and tense.

The birds were setting up a squawking clatter as they approached. In the shelter of the trees was a repeat of the scene on the south fork. Two trappers lay dead.

Travis dismounted, handing his reins to Martin. Venturing into the cool shade of the trees he looked the camp over. There had been a fire, long cold. As before the packs had been scattered in searching them. There had been horses, they were gone. No doubt to carry away the stolen pelts.

The dead men were still in their blankets, which meant the cowards had shot them in their sleep. The blankets had kept the scavengers off at least. He rolled the first man over; he had been shot in the back of the head. He had seen him before, but didn't know his name. Checking the second man, it was Arthur Lakey, better known as Mountain Lion

Lakey because he had yellow eyes. A thing never seen before. He was a friend, who, him and the boys, had many times shared a fire with.

Travis walked back out of the trees to where Martin and Prisque waited.

"Same thing?" Martin asked.

Travis nodded. "I knew them. I swear, I will shoot Luther Monk dead, the first time I see him."

"We should bury them," Martin said.

"Oh, we will. I won't leave a friend to eaten by the varmints."

Pulling shovels from the packs, they began to dig the graves. "You know, I'm gettin' mighty sick of buryin' friends," Travis said angrily.

"We're trying to get them," Prisque said. "They're always two steps ahead of us."

"We have to change that," Travis said.

They finished burying the men. While Prisque put up the shovels, Travis began circling the cottonwoods looking for their trail. Martin followed him.

Travis was disturbed by what he was finding. He had feared this, and now it was happening. They had come in as a group to kill and rob, but that was not how they were leaving this place. "This is bad. This is bad," he kept repeating in a low voice.

"What is?" Martin asked.

He didn't answer Martin until he had made the full

circle back to the horses. Then, he said, with a hint of despair, "They've split the blanket."

"What does that mean?" Martin asked.

"They are leaving in four pairs, each with a pack horse, and going in different directions," Travis said with exasperation. "They've divided the pelts, and the gang split up."

Martin stared at Travis, "We cannot follow four different trails at once."

"No, we can't, and I don't know which one is Monks. It's likely him and Black paired up. If I can only follow one, that's the one I'd follow, but I have no idea which one it is."

"How will they know, without Monk guiding them, how to get to Pierre's Hole?" Martin asked.

"I'm sure, in the past, Monk told them how, to get there. That's why they feel confident enough to break out on their own," Travis replied.

"What should we do?" Martin asked.

Travis stared out across the prairie for a long minute, then said more to himself, then to the others, "They all have to go to the rendezvous to sell the pelts." He looked in the different directions the paired-off trails had gone. "We forget about the trails."

"How will we find them, then?" Martin asked.

Travis mounted the roan, "We're goin' straight to Pierre's Hole, and watch for 'em to show up."

HISTORICAL NOTE

The Pemmican War

The Metis are people of French and Indian blood, mostly Cree and Ojibwe. Their language is a unique blend of French, Cree, and Ojibwe, creating a tongue spoken only among the Metis. Their original homeland was in the southern portions of what became the Canadian provinces of Ontario, and Manitoba. The Lake Winnipeg, Red River, and Assiniboine River area was their mainstay. They were primarily involved in the fur trade and hunting, but were also farmers.

As the British, and English Canadians, began to take over the country, there was a concerted effort to force the Metis out of their homeland, to be taken over by the newcomers. The Pemmican War was an event spurred by that effort.

The forks of the Red and Assiniboine Rivers, had been the traditional fur trading rendezvous location for years. In 1809, the Northwest Fur Company (NWC), built Fort Gibraltar at the forks to conduct their fur trade. The Metis traded, and often worked for the NWC.

Voyageurs who trapped for the NWC in boat brigades, worked from Fort William at Lake Superior. Their staple diet was pemmican, a food made from dried, powdered buffalo meat and tallow, mixed with berries. NWC regularly canoed in fresh pemmican to the voyageurs by way of the Red and Assiniboine river routes. The Metis buffalo hunters supplied the buffalo used by the NWC for the pemmican.

In 1812, Thomas Douglas, the Fifth Earl of Selkirk in Scotland, owned a controlling share of the Hudson Bay Company (HBC). He purchased 116,000 acres of the Red River land from the British government. Land that belonged to the Metis, Cree, Ojibwe, and Assiniboine people. Douglas moved a colony of indentured Scotsmen to the Red River, and settled them in what he called the Red River Colony, an establishment of the HBC. He promised the indentured Red River Colony servants, each, one hundred acres of land after three years. At the same time Douglas' men began building Fort Douglas, an HBC Trading post, on the west side of the Red River. Its purpose, to directly trade against the NWC.

The Red River Colony, needless to say, was not well accepted by the Metis, or Indians. By 1814, the Red River Colony had laid claim to the Metis holdings, requiring them to adhere to the laws of the Colony. The Metis were being denied the freedom to govern themselves, however, they refused to capitulate.

In January, 1814. The Red River Colony Governor, Miles Macdonell, issued the 'Pemmican Proclamation'. The proclamation prohibited the exportation of pemmican outside of the HBC's Red River Colony. The NWC, and the Metis saw the proclamation for what it was, a ploy to starve out the voyageur boat brigades, and destroy the NWC as competition in the fur trade. NWC, and the Metis, defied the proclamation. As the routes on the Red and Assiniboine were blockaded by Fort Douglas, the NWC began to ship pemmican to the brigades overland to Fort William.

By 1815, the bad blood had deepened as the Metis and Colony Scots, harassed each other, and often exchanged gunfire. The Metis demanded that the colonists leave the forks. Macdonell was forced to surrender to NWC representatives, and was sent to Montreal to be tried in court for illegally confiscating pemmican. He was never charged, or sent to court.

In 1816, in retaliation for the NWC, and the Metis, refusing to submit to the proclamation, HBC men seized and destroyed Fort Gibraltar. The tensions heightened to an exploding point.

On June 19, 1816, Cuthbert Grant, Metis leader, and NWC clerk, led a party of 60 mounted Metis, and Indians, past an HBC gunboat blockade at the forks. They were avoiding the Red River Colony, going cross-country, west of Fort Douglas, bound for La Grenouillère, on Lake Winnipeg, to deliver needed pemmican to the NWC voyageurs. HBC Governor, Robert Semple, along with 28 armed HBC men, confronted Grant's group to stop them from making the delivery.

Angry words were exchanged, tempers flared, and one of Semple's men fired on the Metis. Someone from Grant's party fired back. Then, Semple's men opened fire on the Metis, however, as Grant explained later. When Semple's men opened fire, the Metis and Indians dove to the ground. Failing to reload, Semple's men took off their hats and cheered the deaths of the Metis. The Metis stood back up and fired on the HBC men. Then, attacked in hand-to-hand fighting. Inside of 15 minutes, the remaining HBC men fled the fight, leaving 20 dead, including Semple. On Grant's side, one was dead, one wounded. The confrontation became known as the *Battle of Seven Oaks.*

The British government called for an inquiry of the event. Lt. Col. William Coltman was appointed to investigate. He traveled from Montreal to the Red River. His conclusion was that, Semple's man fired the first shot. A second shot was fired from Grant's side, then both sides liberally shot at each other. His finding stated, *"persons of known talents and general information such as the Earl of Selkirk and Governor Semple should have known that their enforcement of the hunting and trading edicts showed a blameable carelessness as to the consequence, on a subject likely to endanger both the peace of the country and the lives of individuals."* He also indicated in his report that, *the pemmican policy was a dangerous policy*. Grant was charged for his part, but the charges were dropped.

On August 12, 1816, Thomas Douglas arrived with 90 soldiers. They captured the NWC headquarters and supply base at Fort Williams. They accused the NWC men of murder, and arrested the officers. They were tried in York, but were all acquitted.

Today the Pemmican War, and the Battle of Seven Oaks, is remembered as the first time the Metis asserted themselves as a free nation, who could trade freely, and govern themselves without outside interference.

ABOUT THE AUTHOR

Mountain men, Voyageurs, pioneers, and explorers make up the branches of Dave's family tree. His mother's side was from Canada where the men plied the fur trade in the Canadian wilderness. Others moved down into the wilds of Northern Minnesota and established trading posts among the Chippewa. They were pioneers in establishing Centerville, Minnesota.

His father was born in 1905, and saw the last of the old west, and his natural grandfather died out West while working as a telegrapher for the railroad. His step-grandfather, born in the 1800's, was Native Blackfoot from Montana. He was a hunter and horseman who brought a great deal of Old West influence into the Fisher family.

As a lifelong Westerner Dave inherited that pioneer blood and followed in the footsteps of his ancestors as a trapper and hunter. Originally from Oregon, he worked cattle and rode saddle broncs in rodeos. His adventures have taken him across the wilds of Alaska as a horse packer and hunting guide, through the Rocky Mountains of

Montana, Wyoming, and Colorado where he wrangled, guided and packed for a variety of outfitters, and the National Park Service.

Dave weaves his experience into each story. His writing, steeped in historical accuracy, and drawing on extensive research, draws his readers into the story by their realism and Dave's personal knowledge of the West, its people, and character.

He also had a run as a performing cowboy poet and western humorous. His venues included performances in Oregon, California, Wyoming, Nebraska, and Texas, as well as, Piper's Opera House, and the Gold Hill Hotel, in historic Virginia City, Nevada;

He has over 500 fiction and non-fiction works published. Included are: Historical western and outdoor novels, cowboy poetry, short stories and short story collections, inclusion in 18 anthologies, and numerous outdoor oriented articles. He has won the *Will Rogers Gold Medallion Award* three times for outstanding Western Fiction. Nine of his short stories have earned Reader's Choice Awards.

Made in the USA
Las Vegas, NV
23 October 2024

10406309R20128